Praise for the A

Editorial Reviews of *The Curse of Gandhari*:

Editor's Pick for October 2019 (*Writersmelon*)

'The most interesting part of the book...is the relationship between Gandhari and Krishna. Banerjee explores the duality of the power hierarchy between the two - Krishna is Gandhi's junior in relation, but she is the devotee and the Lord. The shifting nature of their equation is skillfully examined.' (*The Telegraph India*)

'Women in the Mahabharata have often been misunderstood as passive and non-reactive, which now stands rightfully challenged through creative retelling and interpretation of their choices. This narrative also reveals to us that during that time each woman, possessing a strong individuality and an equally strong viewpoint, had the complete freedom to do what they wanted to do - their choices were independent of the positions of power their families held.' (*Financial Express*)

'The blindfolded queen, mother of the Kauravas in the Mahabharata, is built up in this book as an unconventional heroine of strength and strong will.' (*Pune Mirror*)

Hindu Love Stories

Dharmically Ever After

Aditi Banerjee

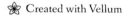

For my parents, who allowed me to read all the love stories I could find;
For my gurus, who teach me how to read the Puranas and the Itihaasa;
For my husband, who teaches me about love every day.

And always for Krishna—

He whose blessings make the dumb eloquent
And the lame cross mountains.

(Mookam karoti vaachaalam pangum langhayate girim;
Yatkripaa tamaham vande paramaanandamaadhavam.)

*When You go off to the forest during the day,
    a tiny fraction of a second becomes like a
    millennium for us because we cannot
    see You. And even when we can eagerly
    look upon Your beautiful face, so lovely
    with its adornment of curly locks, our
    pleasure is hindered by our eyelids,
    which were fashioned by the foolish
    Creator.*

...

*O dearly beloved! Your lotus feet are so soft
    that we place them gently on our breasts,
    fearing that Your feet will be hurt. Our
    life rests only in You. Our minds,
    therefore, are filled with anxiety that
    Your tender feet might be wounded by
    pebbles as You roam about on the forest
    path.*

— From Gopi Gita, the Song of the
Gopis, to Krishna *in the Srimad
Bhagavata* (Translation by
ISKCON)

Contents

Preface   xiii

Part One
Beginnings

1. Ardhanarishvara   3
2. Vishnu & Lakshmi   8
3. The Birth of Radha as a Blind Girl   16

Part Two
Stories of Wooing

4. Agni & Swaha   21
5. The Two Wives of Skanda   31
6. Rukmini & Krishna   40

Part Three
Sometimes Love is Fleeting

7. Menaka & Vishwamitra   53
8. Pururavas & Urvashi   60

Part Four
Kama, Too, Must Be Honored

9. Agastya & Lopamudra   67
10. Kamadeva & Rati   75

Part Five
Devotion

11. Usha & Aniruddha   85
12. Chyavana & Sukanya   92

Part Six
Rising, Not Falling

Note — 103

13. Satyabhama & Krishna — 105
14. Hemachuda & Hemalekha — 112
15. Chaitanya Mahaprabhu & Vishnupriya Devi — 127
16. Bilvamangala Thakur & Chintamani — 134
17. Leela & Padma — 138

Part Seven
Sacrifice

18. Savitri — 149
19. Ruru & Pramadvara — 166
20. The Dust of the Gopis' Feet — 172

Part Eight
Separation

Note — 179
21. The Story of the Crow — 181
22. The Grief of Shiva — 186
23. Separation in Union: The Two Bees — 188
24. Union in Separation: A Story of Radha, Rukmini & Krishna — 194

Part Nine
Leela

Note — 201
25. Peacock Leela — 203
26. The Mock Quarrel of Shiva & Parvati — 207

Part Ten
Bhamati

27. Bhamati — 213

Afterword   219
Notes   225
Bibliography   229
Acknowledgments   237
About the Author   241
Also by Aditi Banerjee   243

Preface

Ya kundendu tushara haara dhavala, ya
*   shubhra vastravrita*
Ya veena vara danda mandithakara, ya
*   shwetha padmaasana*
Ya brahmachyuthaha shankara prabrithibhi
*   devai, sada poojitha*
Samaam paatu saraswathi bhagavathi,
*   nihshesha Jaddyapaha.*

(Salutations to Saraswati Devi, who is pure
*   white like the jasmine flower, with the*
*   coolness of the moon, brightness of snow,*
*   and shine like the garland of pearls, and*
*   who wears a white dress;*
Whose hands are adorned with the veena
*   and the boon-giving staff and who is*
*   seated on a white lotus;*
Who is always adored by Brahma, Vishnu,
*   Shiva and the other Devas.*

*O Devi, please protect me and remove my
ignorance completely.)*

'Hindu love stories' is perhaps an eyebrow-raising topic for a book. In fact, when I first started researching and writing this book, I felt a bit sheepish about the title and concept too. Shouldn't I write about something philosophical, something scholarly and complex, like Vedanta, something aloof from mundane existence?

And the stories here are not what we conventionally think of as 'love stories'. There are no simplistic fairy tales that end in happily-ever-after. Many of the stories are bittersweet or subsume the concept of love into larger discussions of metaphysical and philosophical notions. There is no fluff in these stories, no escapism, no naive promises delivered through rose-colored glasses. Quite the opposite, in fact.

And yet the fact that we do not conceive of such stories as 'love' stories only goes to show how conditioned we have become into thinking of 'love' in only one way—the modern popular culture depictions in romance novels and movies. We do not think of the story of Savitri as a love story, but what can be a higher expression of love than confronting Yama Deva, the God of Death and Justice, to seek her husband's life to be restored?

There are deeper issues at play too. We have been conditioned into a duality of thinking. Spirituality is something distant and rarified; while, here and now, we deal with the practicalities of life, the desires and impulses that drive us, the travails and drama of family life. We have been conditioned to think that spirituality and love cannot co-exist, that they are in inherent conflict. As a result, our attempts at spirituality are tepid and weak; we put it off while we deal with the pesky human affairs that consume our immediate attention. It never occurs to us that we need the teachings of Dharma the most precisely when we are struggling with the trials and travails of samsara.

On top of that, centuries of colonization have burdened Hindus with a deep sense of prudishness and guilt when it comes to matters of the heart. This has resulted in deep-rooted misconceptions and misunderstanding of the traditional Hindu and Indic conceptions of love. This has made us unhealthy and dysfunctional in how we approach relationships and pursue what we consider to be 'love'.

Moreover, with the destruction of the traditional community and societal infrastructure that supported the transmission of Dharmic teachings and values-based education, there now exists a vacuum in which there is little to no Hindu or Dharmic discourse on matters related to family, love, and relationships (at least not in English). We have become alienated from the traditional knowledge and wisdom that helps us to healthily and harmoniously integrate our pursuit of love, with all of its attendant emotional and physical needs and desires, with Dharma and *sadhana*, or spiritual practice.

We have wrongly come to associate Dharma and spirituality exclusively with the path of renunciation and celibacy.

If we were all qualified and ready for the path of renunciation and celibacy; if we were prepared to turn to the path of *nivrtti*, withdrawal from the external world, that would be one thing. But the practical reality is that many of us, most of us, do still have a value for this world and all the joys and sorrows that come into play in this plane of existence. Love still matters to us.

So, whenever we do think and talk about love — and as human beings, we naturally think and talk about it *a lot* —

lacking any readily available alternative, we do so in terms of the modern fairy-tale conceptions of love generated by popular culture, especially in the modern West. We have grown so alienated from our own literary and religious heritage, our own civilizational values, that we think of love and romance as something foreign.

Much of the depression, stress, and mental and emotional problems we face today is because of a fundamental dysfunctionality in orienting our psyche when it comes to matters relating to self-esteem, building meaning and purpose into our lives, and how we approach relationships. Because we lack a basic grounding in the practices and conceptions relating to Dharma, that which holds together and leads to the ultimate wellbeing of not just the individual but all sentient beings in the sense of *loka sangraha*, we are unable to form a coherent mindset and values framework for ourselves that will be conducive to psychological and spiritual wellbeing and growth.

We have come to associate traditional societies with repression. In reality, though, Hinduism is much more frank and open about matters relating to sexuality, desire, and love than we ordinarily perceive. There is not in Hinduism a black-and-white dichotomy between love and the path spiritual.

Rather, there is a nuanced understanding and acceptance of the reality of human feelings and a channeling of that into the guardrails of Dharma which protect against the chaos and destructiveness that can otherwise arise if we heedlessly give in to our baser impulses and urges without restraint. That kind of unmitigated hedonism is destructive for the individual and society — this is not a moral indictment but rather a philosophical understanding of the workings of human nature and an orientation always to prioritize loka sangraha, the wellbeing of the Whole, and create an ecosystem and culture that is conducive to the pursuit of moksha, liberation from the apparent cycle of birth and death, or self-realization.

In Hinduism, love and desire are not to be neglected. The four Purushartha, or principal aims of human life, are, in order, Dharma (the pursuit of that which is appropriate conduct for an individual in any given circumstance; an individual's dharma is in consonance with the larger principle of dharma that upholds the harmony and order of the cosmos as a whole for the sake of *loka sangraha* [the welfare of all sentient beings]), Artha (the pursuit of wealth in accordance with Dharma), Kama (the pursuit of enjoyment in accordance with Dharma), and Moksha (the pursuit of enlightenment / self-realization / liberation). Classical Sanskrit literature and the sacred texts of Hinduism are replete with descriptions of sensuous beauty and amorous interludes. Kamadeva is himself one of the most important Devas of the Hindu pantheon.

But this enjoyment, this sense of enchantment, is tempered with a philosophical understanding of the ultimate ephemeral nature of the play of desire and enjoyment. The stories of Hindu literature that deal with love and romance point us to understand and then transcend this never-ending cycle of desire, temporary fulfillment, the replacement of the first desire with a new, stronger desire once the fulfillment wears off as it inevitably does, and so forth.

The ethos of the Hindu approach to love, exemplified in the stories in this collection from Hindu sacred texts and history, is to seek to harmonize: harmonize the needs and desires of the individual with that of the family and society at large; harmonize love with spirituality; harmonize the paths of *pravrtti* (living a life in the world without becoming of the world, like how the lotus grows out of the mud but is untouched by the mud) and nivrtti, like two wings of a bird.

One example of this approach to harmonize and spiritualize is demonstrated by the Kashi yatra rite that is part of the Hindu wedding rites in certain parts of India. In Hinduism, there are four stages of life: brahmacharya (the phase of youth and celibacy, when the mind is most receptive to being molded, this stage of life is dedicated to education); the grhastha ashrama (the phase dedicated to being a householder, creating and caring for the family, including through marriage); vanaprastha (gradual withdrawal from worldly duties and turning toward inner contemplation and deepening spiritual practices); and finally sannyasa (renunciation).

The marriage ceremony represents the transition from brahmacharya to the grhastha ashrama. Before the wedding, the father of the bride comes across a young man who is on his way to Kashi, the abode of Shiva, the most sacred city for Hindus, to pursue a life of learning and penance. The father approaches him and asks him, young man, consider this daughter of mine to accompany you on the path of Dharma, consider taking her as your bride. He reminds the young man that all the four ashramas or stages of human life must be experienced; one cannot skip ahead to sannyasa without going through the grhastha ashrama (unless one has the samskaras, natural inborn tendencies born of karma from the past).

The father says, in essence, consider taking this daughter of mine to be your partner in Dharma and sadhana; let both of you support each other and help each other grow; let this yatra of marriage lead you to the abode of Shiva, toward the path of moksha.

If the groom agrees, the wedding rites commence. This is not mere playacting; the rites leave a deep impress, subtle yet powerful, on the marriage and the psyches of the couple over the years and decades to come. This specific rite leaves an imprint on both the groom and bride, a reminder that the ultimate purpose of their coming together is to prepare and develop them to eventually attain enlightenment. The Kashi yatra is not abandoned or even postponed; that is still the destination but the way for them is now shaped through the path of marriage.

This collection draws upon stories from the Vedas, from the Itihaasa and the Puranas, the epic literature of Hinduism, some dating back to the mists of time, and also from historical accounts of sadhus, sages, and scholars. I have relied on English translations for my source material, and where possible, I have compared different translations and read them against the original to try to hew as closely as possible to the original text while allowing for some stylistic embellishments.

The Bibliography includes a list of the main sources consulted for each story; I highly recommend reading the primary source versions in whichever language one is comfortable to get the most authentic and unabridged presentation of the stories. My purpose is not to create anything new or add anything to the original; there is nothing to be added. This book is merely an attempt to make accessible to a modern audience texts they may not otherwise read.

After all, our ancestors took a painstaking amount of time and energy to collate these stories, to transmit them through the generations, to embed them into our collective memory as a people. It is part of our duty to honor them by remembering and reflecting upon these tales, not just as lore or 'mythology', but as part of our heritage and identity.

For those who are not vested in Hinduism per se, I believe these stories are still relevant and important. From the perspective of multiculturalism and pluralism, there is value in understanding the indigenous traditions and world-view of an ancient civilization. It is essential to learn different ways of looking at the world and different approaches to addressing universal human experiences, needs and drives. It enriches our own understanding of ourselves and studying the accumulated wisdom of our ancestors only increases the depth and breadth of practices and concepts in our toolkit, so to speak, that we reach into to help improve our lives.

This is by no means a comprehensive collection. There are many more Hindu love stories to retell and share, and perhaps we will be able to do so in future editions or additions to the series.

Part One

Beginnings

1

Ardhanarishvara

Om. In the beginning, or rather, at the time of *a* beginning, Brahma, the Creator, was unhappy with his creation. He stroked his white beard— he came into the world an old man, referred to affectionately and sometimes disparagingly as the Grandfather—and glared at his mind-born sons, the Sanatkumaras. One by one, he looked at the four of them, his eyes emitting sparks of anger.

They returned his gaze serenely. They were immersed in meditation upon Shiva, intent on achieving enlightenment and escaping this *srishti*, this material world of samsara, that he had worked so hard to bring them into. For how many hundreds and thousands of years had he wrought from his brain bits of the activating energy necessary to stimulate life? From the power of his own mind had these sons been born. They were born fully enlightened, fully grown up, and fully unconcerned with the messiness of material life.

This will not do, thought Brahma. *This simply will not do.* He had been given one job to do by Shiva, and if he did not do it properly, Shiva would likely cut one of his five heads off. Brahma urged his sons to become creators in their own right, to bring more sentient beings into the world, but they ignored him and continued to meditate on Shiva.

Brahma began to cry tears of fear and frustration.

He went to Vishnu, reclining on his serpentine bed in the Ksheera Sagara, the Milky Ocean, for help. Vishnu kept his eyes closed as he listened to Brahma's tale of woe. With every exhale, Vishnu breathed worlds into existence.

Brahma frowned to see how effortlessly Vishnu did this —it just flowed out of him, dreams that manifested as living worlds and realms. Brahma would need a millennium just to create one. Vishnu's dreams were beyond Brahma's conception.

Vishnu's breath stirred the cool air, hovering in white wisps above the milky waters of the Ksheera Sagara.

"Go meditate upon Shiva," Vishnu said. And again he fell into a reverie.

Brahma journeyed across that vast white ocean, his feet floating above the rippling tides of milk, eyes trained in concentration upon the pearlescent sky until he

returned to Prithvi, which one day some people would call
Earth. He walked over desert sands and climbed brown
mountains to look upon seas that crashed and foamed,
empty of life forms. He watched cloudless skies, his eyes
following a sun that marched dutifully across the sky and
dropped off the horizon without lingering to create a beautiful sunset. All the mechanical workings of a planet were
present, but it still was not a *world*, not without life, not
without beauty.

Brahma closed his eyes and meditated upon Shiva.
Heat started gathering in his head. It gathered in such
intensity and force that the center of his forehead exploded
and Brahma was almost incinerated into ashes. He managed
to keep hold of himself and when he regained his senses, his
eyes opened to a most astonishing sight.

It was the form of Ardhanarishvara. The right half was
Shiva, and the left half Devi, she who would one day
become Sati and Parvati; she who would one day become
Kali, the dark one, as well as Gauri, the fair one. Shiva was
dark, broad in shoulders and flat in chest, his waist and
thighs muscled. His head bore the crescent moon and the
flowing waters of Ganga. Devi, on the left half, the side
signifying intuition and creation and sentimentality, bore a
full breast and a sweetly curving waist, golden in color.

Brahma understood then that what had been missing
from his mental cogitations, from his meditation and
creation, was the feminine aspect, the principle of Prakriti,
nature, that is needed to complement Purusha, the Primor-
dial One. The cosmos, all of creation, needs the balance of
Shiva and Shakti.

Thence commenced the next phase of creation through
copulation, the joining together of Purusha and Prakriti,
male and female. In every cycle of creation that occurs

through the ages, Ardhanarishvara always appears to catalyze creation.

~

OF COURSE, there is never just one story or one version of a story. The story above is from the Shiva Purana. Other Puranas, like the Skanda Purana, tell us that after they were married, Parvati wanted to experience the ecstasy of Shiva. Shiva, too, wanted to share all that he felt and thought with his wife. Parvati vowed to undertake any kind of austerity needed to enter Shiva's body and being, to experience that which he alone was able to feel.

She said, "Let me reside in you, all the while embracing you limb by limb."

Shiva smiled and said that all she had to do was sit in his lap. Parvati did so, placing her full trust in him, and with complete surrender, she became half of him in the manifestation of Ardhanarishvara.

~

THERE IS YET another story of the appearance of Ardhanarishvara. One day, Shiva and Parvati were sitting together at the top of Mount Kailasha, their icy mountain abode. The devas and rishis, the enlightened sages, all came to offer their obeisance. Except for one rishi, Rishi Bhringi, every Deva and rishi made their *pradakshina*, clockwise circumambulations, around both Shiva and Parvati, as a gesture of reverence for them.

Rishi Bhringi had vowed to worship only Shiva and refused to offer his worship to Shiva's consort. Parvati, angered by his insolence, pronounced a curse that may all of

his flesh and blood disappear. Instantly, the rishi transformed into a beetle covered only with insect skin. He was
unable to even stand.

The ever-compassionate Shiva blessed him with a third
leg so that at least he could keep his balance. The rishi was
so touched at this measure of grace that he danced joyously
with his three legs and sang out praises of Shiva.

Parvati was irritated by this rishi who would not honor
her. She undertook austerities in order to obtain a boon
from Shiva, which he immediately granted, as he could
never refuse his wife. She sought to be united with his body
always, to become inseparable from him, to become his
other half so they would never be considered as two again.
Thus they took the form of Ardhanarishvara and were
joined together as one.

Parvati thought that would be the end of the matter
with the pesky Rishi Bhringi. But *bhakti*, or devotion, too,
knows no limits. Undaunted, Rishi Bhringi, keeping his
beetle form, pierced a small hole through the joined form of
Ardhanarishvara and performed his pradakshina around
Shiva alone. This won the admiration of Parvati, and she
blessed the rishi for his steadfast devotion and unflinching
abidance of his vow.

2

Vishnu & Lakshmi

"The eternal Sri, loyal to Visnu, is the mother of the world. Just as Visnu pervades the universe, O excellent brahmin, so does she. Visnu is meaning; Sri is speech. She is conduct; Hari is behavior. Visnu is knowledge; she is insight. He is Dharma; she is virtuous action. ... Visnu is the creator; Sri is creation. She is the earth and Hari earth's upholder. The eternal Laksmi is contentment, O Maitreya; the blessed lord is satisfaction. Sri is wish, the lord desire. ... Sri is the sky; Visnu, the Self of everything, is wide-open space. Sri's husband is the moon; its beauty is the constant Sri. Laksmi is fortitude, enacted in the world, Hari the all-pervading wind. Govinda is the ocean, O brahmin; Sri is the shore, great seer."[1]

— English translation from Classical Hindu Mythology: A Reader in the Sanskrit Puranas

T his story comes to us from the Vishnu Purana. Once, Durvasa, the temperamental rishi or sage, was wandering across Earth. He beheld an *Apsara* adorned with a garland of flowers so sweet-smelling that he became intoxicated. It is said that the garland had been gifted to her by Sri, otherwise known as Lakshmi, herself. He was so enchanted by the smell of those celestial flowers that he demanded the garland from the Apsara, and she bestowed it upon him. Apsaras tend to be carefree and lighthearted like that.

Continuing along his way, Durvasa met Indra, the king of the Devas. Indra was seated on his elephant, Airavata, and was surrounded by other Devas. Something about the garland had filled the ordinarily grumpy sage with a feeling of friendliness toward others. Seeing Indra, Durvasa smiled and removed from his neck the garland of flowers, now swarming with bees attracted to the ambrosial scent. He threw the garland to Indra.

Indra caught the garland and placed it on Airavata's head.

The smile left Durvasa's face and his brow furrowed thunderously. He had expected Indra to wear the garland himself or at least to bow to him out of respect.

The Devas surrounding Indra stepped back; even they were wary of the rishi's temper. Indra was oblivious to the undercurrents of tension, tipsy as he was.

Durvasa stared at the colorful flowers shining like the Ganga River against the dark gray skin of the elephant, which resembled the stormy Mount Kailasha, the abode of Shiva.

Airavata, overcome by the fragrance of the flowers, eyes

dimmed with inebriety, grasped the garland with his trunk
and tossed it on the ground.

That was when Durvasa lost his temper.

"You! Indra! As always, you are intoxicated with your
own power. Only an idiot like you would not honor such a
gift as I have given you. Do you not know that Sri herself is
manifest in these flowers? You did not bow before me. You
did not wear the garland yourself, which would have
brought you unlimited blessings.

"Now your sovereignty over the three worlds will be
broken. Just as you have cast into the mud and ruined the
garland I gifted you, so, too, shall your reign over the
universe be destroyed."

Indra jumped off the elephant's back and rushed
toward the sage, pressing his body into the dirt in prostra-
tion. He rose and rattled off entreaties and apologies to the
angered rishi. He explained that it was Airavata, after all,
who had discarded the garland—how could Indra be held at
fault?

Durvasa snorted and waved a dismissive hand.
"Everyone knows that one's *vahana*, one's companion and
chariot, is but a reflection of one's own nature and personality. Just as you are drunk, so is he. It is no use asking my
forgiveness. Other rishis may be soft, but remorse is a
stranger to me. Who in the universe can look at my face,
dark with frowns, surrounded by my blazing hair, and not
tremble? No, I will not forgive you."

With that, Durvasa walked away.

Indra climbed on the back of Airavata and traveled back
to his abode, Amaravati. His head hung in defeat. He knew
he was really in trouble this time. Even the king of the
Devas could not mess with a rishi, especially a temperamental one like Durvasa, and go unpunished. He sighed

and entered the chamber of his wife, Shachi. He collapsed onto her bed, anxious about the doom about to befall them all.

Indeed, it did not take long for Durvasa's displeasure to manifest. Within days, all vegetation, all crops, all the flowers and greenery in all the three worlds had withered and died. The sacrificial fires were extinguished. Worship and rites came to a halt. Soon, moral depravation took over humanity. Without the auspiciousness embodied by Sri, how could there be any vitality left in the world? Life itself dried up.

Indra and all the Devas grew feeble. The enemies of the Devas, the Asuras, took advantage of the situation. The Devas were defeated and fled for refuge to Brahma, who you may remember was the Creator among the Devas.

Hutashana, or Agni Deva, the God of Fire, led the procession to Brahma. Brahma tugged at his beard and wrinkled his nose. This was a big problem. And when there were big problems, he did as all good workers do and delegated up to the big boss, which in this case was Vishnu.

Brahma, Vishnu, and Shiva constitute the trinity in charge of Creation (Brahma), Preservation (Vishnu), and Dissolution (Shiva). When the world is in crisis, when the Devas are in danger, Vishnu comes to the rescue.

Brahma led the Devas to the northern shore of the Ksheera Sagara, the Milky Ocean, where Vishnu was reclining on a serpentine bed under the cover provided by the thousand-headed hood of Shesha, the king of the Nagas. Each of Shesha's heads bore the weight of a planet. It is said that the base of Shesha is located in the depths of Patala Loka, the lowest and darkest of the worlds. From there, he holds up Earth and all the other worlds. Upon him, Vishnu reclines as they float on the vast ocean of bliss known as the Ksheera Sagara.

Brahma cleared his throat and began singing hymns of praise to Vishnu. The words he chanted were quite poetic and beautiful. After all, he was used to offering paeans to Vishnu to rescue him from this or that problem. So, he had gotten a lot of good practice by now.

After Brahma finished, the rest of the Devas also cried out their pleas for good measure. "We bow down to that glorious nature which Brahma himself does not know," they said, and even Brahma nodded along with those lines. After the Devas, the rishis prayed to Vishnu, too, a bit more calmly. The end of the universe did not faze the enlightened ones, after all.

The rishis intoned in somber voices, blended together into a sonorous harmony:

"We bow down to the one being entitled to adoration, he who was there before the beginning, he who was the creator of the Creator. Have pity upon your devotees who are prostrated before you. Here is Brahma; here is Shiva, the three-eyed one, with the Rudras; here is Pusha, the God of the Sun, with the Adityas; and here is Agni Deva, the God of Fire, with all the mighty luminaries; here are the sons of Ashvini; here bow the Vasus and all the winds, the Sadhyas, the Vishvadevas, and Indra, the King of the Gods—all of whom bow before you, all the tribes of the immortals, seeking succor from you."[2]

Vishnu opened his eyes and smiled. He comforted them and promised that their energies and vitality would soon be restored. Sri, or Lakshmi, had indeed disappeared from the world with the casting down of the garland and Durvasa's resultant curse, but she would emerge again if they followed his plan. The Devas immediately agreed.

Following Vishnu's instructions, the Devas entered into a truce with the Asuras. They agreed to work together to bring forth Amrita, the nectar of immortality, through the churning of the milky ocean. The Devas and the Asuras collected various medicinal herbs and offered them into the Ksheera Sagara. The waves of the milky sea were radiant as the shining clouds of autumn.

The time for the Samudra Manthan, the churning of the ocean, had come. Together, the Devas and the Asuras churned the ocean by using the sacred mountain, Mandara, as the staff and Shesha's brother, Vasuki the serpent, as the cord. The Devas stood at the tail of the enormous Vasuki and the Asuras at his head. This was the problem with the Asuras — their ego got in the way and they wanted to always be at the top of things.

But this backfired on them badly. The flames emitted from Vasuki's hood scorched the Asuras, burning them, while his breath sent misty clouds toward his tail, reviving the devas with refreshing showers.

Vishnu himself took the form of a tortoise to support the mountain as it was whirled around during the churning. With one portion of his energy, he sustained Vasuki; with another, he energized the Devas. Slowly, the churning went on.

After some time, wondrous things began emerging from the milky waters. First arose the divine cow, Surabhi, duly worshipped by the Devas. As all the celestial beings watched from the skies, Varuni, the Goddess of Wine, appeared, eyes rolling drunkenly. Then came the Parijata tree, perfuming the world with its blossoms. The Apsaras, the celestial beauties gifted with extraordinary talents for music and dancing, shimmered and rose above the frothy foam of the milk, followed by the cool-rayed moon. Shiva seized the moon for himself, tucking it into his hair.

Because there must always be balance in all things, *halahala*, that most terrible of poisons, also fumed out from the sea. Shiva drank it up and held it in his throat, protecting the rest of creation from the toxic poison, and the Nagas, the serpentine deities, also took possession of a share of it.

At long last, Dhanvantari, the medicinal Deva, robed in white, bearing the cup of Amrita in his hands, stood on top of the waves, delighting all the assembled ones with the sight of the nectar of immortality.

Finally, arose Sri, seated on a pink lotus, holding a water lily in her hand. The sight of her enraptured even the rishis, so entrancing was she. The rishis sang hymns of praise to her. The Apsaras danced before her.

The seven sacred rivers came forth to bathe her. The celestial elephants took golden bowls filled with the pure waters and poured them over Lakshmi. Varuna, the god of the sea, presented her with a garland of never-fading flowers, and thus she also became known as the daughter of the sea. Vishwakarma, the artisan of the devas, adorned her with golden ornaments.

Everyone who saw her desired her. The Devas, the Asuras, all gazed upon her with adoration. After being bathed and adorned, Lakshmi finally lifted her eyes. Her eyes fell directly upon the blue chest of Vishnu, and she cast herself upon it, making it her abode. It is for this reason that Vishnu is also known as Srinivasa, the residing place of Sri. From the locus of his heart, Lakshmi turned her eyes upon all the others. The Devas were bewitched by her sight and stood unmoving before her gaze.

Thus were the three worlds again restored to happiness

and thus did Indra regain his power, once the Devas obtained the Amrita. Seated upon his throne and reigning once more in the heavens of Swarga, Indra offered a heart-felt hymn of praise to Lakshmi.

He concluded the beautiful hymn: "The tongues of Brahma are unqualified to celebrate your excellence. Be propitious to me, O lotus-eyed Devi, and never forsake me again."

Sri, the one who abides in all creatures, smiled at Indra, the one who had performed a hundred rites. She offered him two boons of his choosing.

Indra requested that the three worlds never be deprived of her presence. His second request was that she never forsake one who praised her with the hymn he had composed for her. Lakshmi promised that she would never abandon the three worlds again and that she would never leave one who offers her, morning and night, the hymn that Indra had sung to her.

3

The Birth of Radha as a Blind Girl

Vaikuntha and Goloka are two nitya dhamas, imperishable realms immune to the ravages of time. According to Gaudiya Vaishnavism, Krishna resides in Vaikuntha in the form of the four-armed Vishnu and simultaneously presides over Goloka in his two-armed form as Krishna with Radha at his side.

The time had come for Krishna to descend to Earth in his avatara form, to be born as a human and rid the world of demons in preparation for the Kali Yuga, the fourth and most degenerate age of the four-age cycle of time. All the heavenly realms were abuzz, different Devas preparing for their own incarnations to accompany Krishna on his quest.

Krishna asked his beloved Radha to also arrange for her descent unto Earth. But Radha was unwilling to come to Earth, where she would be surrounded by so many people and not always be able to see Krishna. Krishna cajoled her and she finally agreed under one condition—that Krishna would be the first person she would see on Earth.

And so it was that Radha was born to Vrishabhanu and his wife, Kirtida. They were overjoyed to look upon this golden-complexioned sweet child. As they counted her fingers and toes, as their fingers stroked her petal-soft dimpled cheeks, they realized that her eyes were screwed closed. Try as they might, she would not open her eyes.

Days passed, and still Radha would not open her eyes. Some say that five years passed like this. Vrishabhanu and Kirtida were devastated that their daughter could not see. Reports spread throughout Vraj of the beauty and charm of baby Radha. Everyone came to have her darshan, to behold her in front of their eyes. Nanda Maharaja and Yashoda, the parents of Krishna, also came along with their son.

They were good friends with Vrishabhanu and Kirtida. Nanda Maharaja and Vrishabhanu embraced, as did Yashoda Mata and Kirtida. While they were thus occupied greeting each other and discussing the birth of Radha, the little boy, Krishna, quietly climbed down from his mother's lap and toddled into the room where Radha was sleeping.

He knew that she was waiting for him. He climbed onto the bed and gently placed the palm of his right hand over her closed eyes. As soon as she felt his touch, the baby girl opened her eyes to look upon her beloved Krishna.

Noticing that Krishna had escaped, the two sets of parents ran into the room. When they saw that Radha's eyes had finally opened, all rejoiced.

Part Two

Stories of Wooing

4

Agni & Swaha

Agni do I invoke—the one placed to the fore,
god and priest of the sacrifice, the Hotar,
most richly conferring treasure.

Agni, to be invoked by ancient sages and by
the present ones — he will carry the gods
here to this place.

By Agni one will obtain wealth and pros-
perity every day, glorious and richest in
heroes.

O Agni, the sacrifice and rite that you
surround on every side — it alone goes
among the gods.

Agni, the Hotar with a poet's purpose, the
real one possessing the brightest fame,
will come as a god with the gods.

When truly you will do good for the pious
man, o Agni, just that of yours is real, o
Aṅgiras.

We approach you, o Agni, illuminator in the

> *evening, every day with our insight,*
> *bringing homage—*
> *(You), ruling over the rites, the shining*
> *herdsman of the truth, growing strong in*
> *your own home.*
> *Like a father for a son, be of easy approach*
> *for us, o Agni. Accompany us for our*
> *well-being.[1]*

> — English translation of the first
> hymn of the Rg Veda

T he first hymn of the Rg Veda is dedicated to Agni, the Deva of Fire, the messenger of the devas, the eternal purifier, the first among the Devas to be worshiped. And so the story of Agni and Swaha, the Devi who became his consort and wife, also traces back to the Vedas.

In the Upanishads, Swaha represents shakti, the power that cannot be burned by Agni. She is enamored with Agni and longs to be united with him, wishing to dwell with him always. The other Devas notice this and state that the oblations made to Agni will hence be offered while uttering 'Swaha' so that Swaha may always dwell with Agni. That is why even today, when performing *yajna*, the fire sacrifice, each time a drop of ghee or a piece of *samagri* is offered to Agni in the *havan kunda* (fire pit), such oblation is punctuated with the word 'Swaha'.

The Mahabharata elaborates upon this story from the Upanishads. In fact, many of the stories from the Puranas and Upanishads are recounted with variation in the Mahabharata. During the Vana Parva, for example, the Pandavas spend a large part of their thirteen-year exile in the forests and ashrams with the company of rishis. The rishis regale them with stories of their ancestors, of other holy persons, of renowned incidents from history, to help them cope with their ordeal and learn lessons that will strengthen and prepare them for the terrible war to come.

One such story, the story of Agni and Swaha, is narrated by Markandeya Rishi to the Pandavas, the five brothers who are the heroes of the Mahabharata. Swaha was the daughter of Daksha, who was also the father of Sati, Shiva's wife. Swaha had long been in love with Agni and had in fact been pursuing him. But Agni did not even notice her.

Agni was present at every *yajna*. He bore witness to every rite. And so it was that he also presided over the sacrificial rites performed by the *Saptarishi*, the seven great rishis of Hinduism. When the fire had been ignited and the offerings sanctified, Agni took the offerings with him and conveyed them to the respective Devas in Deva Loka, the realm of the gods. As he returned from making the deliveries, he witnessed the wives of the Saptarishi sleeping on their beds.

Agni was enchanted. Their complexions shone like moonbeams, their cheeks like fiery flames. He fell in love with each and every one of them. It is perhaps not so surprising that one of the most exalted devas, he who was inextricably bound up with rites and sacrifice, would fall for the noblest of women wed to the most attained of sages who were devoted to sacrifice and worship.

Agni, the great purifier, was troubled by the impurity of his own thoughts. He recognized that he could not fulfill his own desires. The women he loved were loyal wives to the rishis. He vowed to himself that he would not touch them if they did not desire it. Unable to completely forsake them, though, Agni instead decided to become manifest as their *garhapatya*, their household fire. That way, he could watch them to his heart's content every day.

Only through the contact of that small fire that burned in their homes did Agni connect with the seven women. He stayed like that for a long time, charmed by their virtue, filled with an intense love for them. Neither could he win their hearts, nor could he leave them. Despite the raging flames of longing within himself, Agni ever remained the calmest and most collected of the Devas.

Finally, disgusted with himself and despairing of the situation, Agni retreated to the Chitraratha Forest. He was determined to destroy himself.

Swaha breathed a sigh of relief. Now she saw her chance to win him over. She had been trying to capture his attention for a long time, waiting for a moment of weakness that never came. Until now.

Swaha sympathized with Agni's plight, as she, too, was suffering from unrequited love. She thought of a way to satisfy them both—she would disguise herself as the wives of the Saptarishi. Then he would not be able to turn her away, and she would finally have him to herself.

Swaha's first target was Siva, the wife of Angiras. Angiras is a fascinating rishi in his own right, whose story we will have to explore in a different book. Suffice it to say for now that he was a great rishi.

In the guise of Siva, the wife of Angiras, Swaha approached Agni. She referred to his lovelorn state and announced that she was as tortured by longing as he was. She asked Agni to woo her and vowed that if he did not, she would destroy herself. She told him that she had come under instruction of the other six wives of the Saptarishi.

Agni was skeptical. How could she know of his desire when he had been so careful to hide it? And how would the other six wives have come to known?

Swaha in the form of Siva said, "You have always been our favorite, but we feared you. Now that we have divined your true feelings, it was decided that I should approach you. Accept me, O Agni; my sisters-in-law are waiting and I must return to them soon."

Agni joyfully took Swaha in his arms, taking her to be Siva. They spent an idyllic time together in the forest. In between bouts of lovemaking, Swaha reflected that if anyone were to look upon them in the forest, they would unfairly blame the wife of Angiras for infidelity. She decided to take the form of a bird and fly away from the forest undetected after their tryst.

She left for the White Mountain and took with her the seed she held from her lovemaking with Agni. Seed received during a woman's season was not to be wasted.

The White Mountain was a fearful place. It was guarded by strange seven-headed serpents whose very looks were poisonous. Rakshasas (fearsome male demonic creatures who prowl during the night and generally torment innocent beings) and Rakshasis (female version of Rakshasas) covered the mountain. Swaha quickly climbed up the mountainside and threw the seed into a golden lake.

Swaha returned to the forest to Agni's side and one by one took the forms of the other wives of the Saptarishi. But she could not assume the form of Arundhati. Arundhati was such a powerful ascetic with unmatchable devotion to her husband that Swaha could not impersonate her.

Was Agni completely fooled by Swaha, or did he suspect that there was some ruse even after he had challenged her the first time? After all, he had lived in the

households of each of the seven women, in their most intimate and unguarded of spaces, and watched them day in
and day out for so long. The answer to that we will never
know.

One by one, Swaha deposited into that golden lake the
semen of Agni, taken from each of the six times she had
assumed the form of one of the Saptarishis' wives.

That deposit of semen in the powerful lake produced a
male child of incredible strength and radiance. This
happened on the first lunar day of the month. He had six
faces; twelve ears, hands, and feet; one neck; and one stom-
ach. The child became known as Skanda, among many
other names.

On the second lunar day, Skanda's body was formed.
On the third day, he grew to the size of a small child. On the
fourth day, he developed his limbs. Surrounded by masses
of red clouds flashing lightning, he shone like the sun rising
from the midst of fiery crimson clouds.

Skanda was so powerful, so fierce, that his very appearance shook up the foundations of the universe. The nature
of duality, such as male and female, heat and cold, were
reversed. The planets trembled. Even the rishis grew
anxious at the suffering befalling the sentient beings.

And those who used to live in Chitraratha Forest said to
themselves and to whoever else would listen, "This misery
has been brought about by Agni consorting with the six
wives of the seven great rishis." Others, who had seen
Swaha disguised as the bird, said, "This calamity has been
brought about by a bird."

When the rishis heard about the child said to be the son
of their six wives, they immediately abandoned their wives.
Other than, of course, Arundhati whose form had never
been assumed.

No one imagined Swaha as the source of all the trouble. She, having heard about the birth of Skanda, went to him and revealed to him that she was his mother. She went to the rishis, too, and told them again and again that the child was hers, that their wives were not his mother. All to no avail, as the rishis did not believe her.

But there was one witness who knew the entire truth, a great rishi who was not one of the Saptarishi. That great rishi, Vishwamitra, had attended the sacrifice performed by the Saptarishi when Agni had first become attracted to their wives. He had then followed Agni and realized the truth of his feelings and all that had followed.

Vishwamitra approached Skanda after discovering his whereabouts. With his own hands, Vishwamitra performed all the auspicious rites to be conducted for newly born children. He sang praises of the six-faced Skanda and worshiped the cock, Skanda's vahana, or animal companion and vehicle, and Devi, both of them the first followers of Skanda. The great rishi and Skanda thereby developed a close bond.

Vishwamitra also insisted to the rishis that their wives were perfectly innocent. But the rishis would not reverse their decision to abandon their wives.

The Devas and the other celestial beings feared the powerful new child and asked Indra to kill him. They had already seen the destructive impact Skanda wrought by his mere appearance.

Indra was perplexed. As it happened, he had been looking for someone to appoint as the military commander of the Devas. And he was beginning to think this child would make an excellent choice. Indra refused the request of the Devas, which was uncharacteristic of him, as he was always up for a good fight.

The Devas grumbled at his intransigence. They canvassed among themselves and summoned the six wives of the rishis who Swaha had impersonated. The Devas knew those exalted women could generate a tremendous amount of energy. The women, already abandoned by their husbands, were instructed to kill the child. They bowed and acceded to the request.

When the women encountered Skanda at the base of the White Mountain, however, the already dejected women became even more demoralized. How could they bring themselves to hurt this innocent, radiant child? They approached him.

In pleading voices, they said, "O mighty being, become our adopted son. We are full of affection for you and desire to be your mother. We have been wrongfully cast away by our husbands and suffer from infamy through no fault of our own." Milk oozed out of their breasts as they were overcome by love for him.

Skanda honored them and nursed at their breasts with his six mouths. Then he saw his father, Agni, approaching. Skanda bowed to him. Agni was also full of affection for his son and ran around the world to find suitable toys to gift his child. He soon came back to the White Mountain and played happily with Skanda.

Presently, Indra also came to visit Skanda. Skanda regarded him with a wary eye. So many people were approaching with this or that request. He was growing up fast.

"What is it that you want?" Skanda asked Indra.

Indra explained that there was a situation going on with the stars of the night sky. Abhijit, the younger sister of Rohini, one of the constellations, had become jealous of

Rohini's seniority. She had abandoned the skies and took refuge in the woods to engage in austerities. Now Indra was having a difficult time finding a replacement for the fallen constellation.

Skanda nodded. He understood. He turned to his six nurse-mothers. They were also known as the Krittikas and he had accordingly also become known as Kartikeya, or the son of the Krittikas. He looked at them with his shining dark eyes, and they also understood. They nodded in agreement.

And so it was that the Krittikas were assigned a place in the heavens, forming the Krittika constellation, corresponding to Pleiades in Western astronomy. That constellation, presided over by Agni, even today shines as if with seven heads. And in those distant cold skies, Agni is united with those seven women who enchanted him for so long.

Finally, Swaha approached Skanda. Since he had been so generous to all the others, perhaps he would favor her too.

She said to him, "You are my natural-born son. I desire just one thing from you, which shall grant me exquisite happiness."

Skanda smiled. "What kind of happiness do you wish to enjoy?"

Swaha replied, "O mighty being, I have long been in love with your father, Agni, the God of Fire. But he does not even understand my feelings, let alone reciprocate them. I just wish to live with him forever as his wife."

Skanda closed his eyes for a moment and thought it over.

Then he looked upon her and intoned solemnly, "From this day forth, all the oblations that virtuous men, who do not swerve from the path of Dharma, offer to the Devas or to the pitris, the forefathers, with the incantation of sacred hymns, will be coupled with your name, Swaha, when poured into the fire, presided over by Agni. And thus, you will always live in the presence of Agni, the God of Fire."

Swaha was delighted and she honored both her son and her new husband.

5

The Two Wives of Skanda

As we saw in the previous story, Skanda has a most unusual origin story and is of uncommon power and strength, even among the Devas. It is only meet, therefore, that his consorts and wives and the stories of their union be equally extraordinary. In northern India, Skanda is usually shown as celibate. Many Sanskrit texts, though, describe him as being wed to Devasena. In southern India, he is depicted with two wives, Devasena and Valli. Let us start with the story of Devasena.

Some say that Devasena was raised by Airavata, Indra's beloved elephant. Others say she was Indra's adopted daughter. The Mahabharata tells us that Devasena and Daityasena were both daughters of Daksha. Once while the two sisters were resting on the banks of Manasa Lake, an Asura named Keshi abducted them. He wanted to marry them. Devasena refused, while Daityasena consented.

In the meantime, the Devas were defeated in a battle

with the Asuras. A weary Indra discovered the captured daughters of Daksha. He rescued Devasena. She was understandably shaken by the ordeal and begged her adoptive father to find her a husband who could protect her and defeat the Devas, the Asuras, and the Yakshas, who are male nature spirits.

Devasena asked for a *pati*, the Sanskrit term for a husband, and this gave Indra an idea. The Devas badly needed a commander-in-chief to lead them. A Devasena was the army of the Devas, and a Devasenapati would also be the commander of the army of the Devas. Indra smiled at the fortuitous pun. A husband for Devasena and a commander for the other Devasena

Indra went to Brahma, the Creator Deva, for a consultation. They both agreed that a new Deva had to be born who would serve both as the husband of Devasena and the commander-in-chief of the army of the Devas. Who better to be the father than Agni, the God of Fire? And you will recall the twists and turns taken for that son to be born of Agni from our previous story.

Ultimately, Skanda did become the Devasenapati in both senses of the word—the commander of the army of the Devas as well as the husband to Indra's daughter, Devasena. This type of marriage, where the father (here, Indra) gives away his daughter to a suitable groom, is considered the epitome of a Dharmic marriage in accordance with the Vedas. This is the Brahma form of Hindu marriage that we will read about later.

Skanda's union with Valli, his second wife, is in many ways the complete opposite and represents the other side of the coin—an earthy, passionate romance full of wooing.

THIS VERSION of the story of Valli comes from the Kanda Purana, which is the Tamil version of the Sanskrit text of the Skanda Purana.

In ancient times, the mountainous parts of southern India were under the dominion of various tribes. The chief of the Kuravar tribe, Nambirajan, and his wife prayed to Skanda for a daughter. Their prayers were answered in a most unusual way. On a nearby mountainside, an ascetic named Shivamuni was practicing austerities. One day, a doe passed by. The *muni*, or sage, was so entranced by her beauty that the deer became pregnant just from his gaze.

A girl was born of the doe, and the poor animal, not knowing what to do with a human child, left her in a pit that had been dug out by women searching for sweet potatoes. The baby started crying for milk after the deer ran away. At that time, Nambirajan was passing through the area with his wife and soldiers.

Nambirajan and his wife were charmed by the sight of the young girl. She wore earrings, indicating she was a divine child. They plucked her out of the pit and lovingly named her Sundaravalli or Valli for short. *Valli* was the name for sweet potato roots. They adopted her as their own daughter.

As was tradition among the tribes of the region, when Valli turned twelve years old, she went off to the millet fields. She sat on a wooden platform elevated above the fields and chased parrots, pigs, and other animals away from the crops. She was also ever engaged in prayer and meditation upon Skanda, the beloved Deva of the hunters, whom she loved and wished to attain as her husband.

The great rishi, Narada Muni, happened to come across Valli one day during his travels. He went to Skanda to inform him about this spirited girl of exceptional beauty and devotion. Skanda smiled, delighted that it was time for him to meet his beloved Valli at last.

Skanda arrived, disguised as a hunter, at the millet field Valli was guarding. He spoke to Valli, asking about her home and family. But before he could get very far, Nambirajan and other hunters of the tribe brought food for Valli. They lavished her with plates of honey, millet flour, yam roots, mangoes, and milk.

Skanda took the form of a neem tree and hid from their view, waiting for Valli to be alone again. When her father and the others had left, Skanda approached her and told her he wanted to love her.

Valli was shocked. She looked away from him.

She said, "It would be inappropriate for one like you to love a woman from the lowly hunter tribe."

They heard in the distance drumming and the blaring of horns, a wild frenetic outpouring of music. Valli warned him that the approaching hunters would harass him. Skanda then disguised himself as an old man, a devotee of Shiva.

While in the last story we read about Agni fathering Skanda, it is really Shiva and Parvati who are considered the parents of Skanda. Other stories, which we do not have space to cover here, address how he came to be their child. Suffice it to say that Skanda is always dear to those who are devoted to Shiva and those who are devoted to Shiva are always dear to Skanda.

The hunters, who were all followers of Shiva, bowed to him respectfully. Nambirajan was particularly delighted to have an ascetic devoted to Shiva in their midst.

"Swami! You can stay with my daughter here." He took him to Valli and made all the arrangements for the old man's comfortable stay. Then, the hunters, including Valli's father, left.

Skanda was quite pleased by this turn of events. He asked Valli for food. She put into his hands a portion of millet flour mixed with honey. Then, he said he was thirsty.

"Swami!" Valli said. "If you travel to the seventh mountain after this one, you will see a clear stream. You can drink from there."

The old man's face fell. "My dear girl! I am new here. I may get lost if I go by myself. Come with me."

Valli rolled her eyes but gamely led him to the forest pond in that faraway mountain. With the palms of her hand, she offered him water to drink.

Skanda gazed at her adoringly and said, "Now that you have satisfied my hunger for food and my thirst for water, do also satisfy my craving for you."

Valli was startled. "Swami! What did you say? These words are not appropriate for a devotee of Shiva. You are a great sage. I am born in a tribal family. I took you as my father, since you are so old, and I made the mistake of following you here." She cast her eyes downward. "I'm going back to my post now to guard our millet fields."

She began walking away.

Skanda was running out of ideas. There was only one being he trusted who was quick-witted enough to help him out of this one. He invoked his brother, Ganesha, and asked for his assistance. Ganesha immediately understood the situation and approached Valli in the form of a maddened elephant.

Valli took one look at him and shrieked. She ran into the waiting arms of Skanda in his old-man disguise. She had always been afraid of elephants. She tightened her arms around Skanda and cried out, "Swami! Please save me from the elephant chasing me!"

Skanda hugged her back, shielding her from his brother. He whispered to Ganesha, "Brother, because of you, Valli has come back to me. I have gotten what I have desired. You may go now."

With that, Ganesha disappeared. Then, Skanda showed Valli his real form. She was awestruck at the sight of his six faces and twelve hands as he sat proudly on his peacock mount. She fell at his feet, choked up with emotion.

He raised her up and spoke to her tenderly. "Valli, you were the daughter of Vishnu in your previous birth. You meditated on me with a desire to marry me. I asked you to come to Earth and wait for me. In this birth, you have become the daughter of Nambirajan. I came here only to see you. Very soon, I shall marry you in the presence of all."

Valli was ecstatic at having achieved her dream. She told her closest girlfriends about what had happened and waited for Skanda to marry her, meditating upon him all the while. She returned to the fields to get ready for the harvest.

As time passed, Valli grew moody. She could not speak to anyone. She could not eat properly. She was immersed in thoughts of her beloved and grew thinner and thinner. Skanda came in search of her. He could not find her in the fields and became anxious. After searching the area, he arrived at Nambirajan's house.

Valli's closest girlfriend saw him approaching the house and rushed to intercept him. She told him that if he wanted to keep Valli alive, he would have to take her away now. Valli was unable to bear the separation any longer and was growing weak.

Skanda readily agreed.

The friend went into the house and fetched Valli.

Valli fell at Skanda's feet and pleaded with him to take her away: "If my family sees you now, there will be a big fight. Please take me away to your place."

Skanda brought her to the Thanigai mountains. They rejoiced in their solitude and spent an interlude of time together, relishing each other's company.

Valli's parents worried that she had been kidnapped and sent soldiers to search for her. They came upon the couple enjoying themselves in a mountainside garden. Valli panicked as she saw her father and his men approach them angrily. She tugged on Skanda's arm, worried about what was to come.

Skanda comforted her. "Valli! Do not worry! I shall keep us safe."

Nambirajan and the others of the tribe waged a ferocious attack on Skanda. Skanda merely glanced at his flag, which bore the image of a cock. When Skanda looked at the cock, he jumped up and gave a long crowing. That harrowing sound was enough to shock Nambirajan and all of his men so that they promptly fell down dead.

Narada Muni appeared and bowed before Skanda. "O Deva! Is it appropriate for you to kill Nambirajan and his soldiers, taking away his daughter like this? You must bring them back to life!"

Skanda thought about it for a moment and turned to Valli. He asked her to do it, since it was within her powers to bring them all back to life herself. She closed her eyes and thought only of Skanda. She prayed that her father and all of his soldiers should be revived. She opened her eyes and they immediately woke up, as if they had just been sleeping.

Nambirajan understood what had transpired and recognized the true identity of Skanda. He insisted on hosting a proper wedding in the presence of everyone. Narada conducted the marital rites. Devas congregated in Swarga, the heavens, to witness the wedding of Skanda with Valli. They showered flowers upon the couple.

AFTER THE FESTIVITIES ENDED, Skanda brought Valli back to Thanigai mountain. She realized that the mountain was of significance to Skanda and asked him to describe its importance to her. Skanda explained that while he resides in many different mountains, Thanigai is his favorite abode. After he had defeated Shurapadma and other Asuras, he had taken rest on this mountain. It had cooled the rage within him.

At first, the mountain had been called Cheruttani —*cheru* means "anger" and *ttani* means "to cool down." The mountain had refreshed him and made him calm and cool with kindness. In honor of Skanda, Indra arranged that three blue flowers would blossom in a stream flowing from the mountain: one in the morning, one in the afternoon, and one more in the evening. Indra himself worshiped Skanda three times a day with these flowers.

It is said that anyone who sees this mountain and worships it will be rid of all their sins. If people stay on the mountain for five days, they will obtain all their desires. One's meditations on this mountain will become tenfold in strength and merits. Even the Devas come to worship Skanda on this mountain.

Skanda installed a *vigraha*, an image suitable for worship, of Shiva on the mountain and worshiped him. He stayed with Valli on the mountainside for some time before leaving with her for Kandapuri, Skanda's abode.

WHEN THEY REACHED the entrance of Kandapuri, Devasena welcomed them. He introduced his two wives to each other, took them arm by arm, one on each side of him, and entered the city.

He explained to them, "Both of you were Vishnu's daughters in your previous birth. Both of you wanted to marry me and meditated on me. I had asked you two to wait and I promised to come at the right time to marry you. Amritavalli was born as Devasena, daughter of Indra, and married me. Sundaravalli was born to sage Shivamuni and grew up as Valli, in the home of Nambirajan, and fell in love with me."

Devasena hugged Valli. They lived together in harmony, just as the flower coexists with fragrance, and stayed together with their husband to bless all of the devotees.

It is said that Valli, the innocent daughter of the mountain tribe, she with the creeper-like waist, is the one at whom one of the six faces of Skanda is always smiling in serenity.

In this story, we find harmonization of the refined Vedic form of marriage (represented by Devasena and Skanda) with the earthy, passionate style of marriage (represented by Valli and Skanda). Also, there is a bringing together of the Shaiva aspect, represented by Skanda's parents, Shiva and Parvati, with the Vaishnava aspect, represented by Vishnu who is treated as the parent of both wives of Skanda. Not only that, but even Indra, the king of the Devas, is also swept into the story as the adoptive father of Devasena.

6

Rukmini & Krishna

I t was time for the young princess, Rukmini, to get married. She was the only daughter of King Bhishmaka, the ruler of Vidarbha, and the youngest of his six children. She was the most desirable of brides. The Srimad Bhagavata tells us that Krishna himself thought her a fitting bride for himself, as she was the embodiment of intelligence, generosity, beauty, and agreeability in spirit.

Visitors to Vidarbha regaled her with stories of Krishna. Hearing of the extraordinary beauty, strength, and virtues of Krishna, Rukmini decided that he would be the most suitable husband for her. Rukmi, her eldest brother, detested Krishna and decided in the meantime to marry her off to his friend Shishupala, the king of the Chedi.

Rukmini was not a meek princess. She took matters into her own hands and sent her own proposal to Krishna, the one she intended to marry. She sent a trusted *brahmana*, one devoted to the gathering and sharing of knowledge and the performance of religious rites, as a messenger to Krishna in Dwaraka.

The messenger was granted permission to enter the

palace, and he beheld Krishna seated on a golden throne. Krishna worshiped the brahmana. After the brahmana was fed lunch, Krishna sat next to him and rubbed his feet. He inquired after the brahmana's well-being.

Krishna said, "I salute again and again holy men who are satisfied with what they get, who are devoted to their *svadharma* (their individual dharma), who are friendly to all beings, who are egoless, whose minds are always immersed in me. I hope that the ruler of your country is helpful to you in all ways. Dear to me is a king whose subjects are well-governed and live happily."

Such is the compassion of Krishna. Bhagavan himself massaged the feet of a brahmana and looked after him, feeding him lunch. Indeed, no one is dearer to Sri Krishna than those who are devoted to the paths of bhakti (devotion) and *jnanam* (wisdom).

The brahmana was intent on his mission and without further delay recited from the letter he had been entrusted to convey from Rukmini:

"Hearing about your virtues, which is in itself blissful to the listener, and hearing also about the beauty of your form, my mind, O Achyuta, the immovable one—my mind has entered into you, overcoming all feelings of shyness! O, granter of moksha, freedom from the cycle of birth and death! O noblest among men! Which girl of marriageable age would not choose you for a husband, who are well-matched to her in nobility of birth, character, form, education, youth, wealth, and glory?

"I have therefore chosen you as my husband and have offered myself to you, O, all-pervading one! Accept me as your wife. O, lotus-eyed one! Do not allow the Chedi king to take me away. . . .

"If I have acquired any merit through prayer; through

the practice of sacrifice, charity, religious rites; and through the honoring of the devas, holy men, elders, and teachers; then may my hand not be taken in marriage by anyone other than Krishna—never by anyone else, including Shishupala.

"On the occasion of my marriage arranged for tomorrow, I entreat that you present yourself, surrounded by your generals and armies. After defeating the armies of the kings of Chedi and Magadha, do capture and marry me by force according to the Rakshasa form of marriage. Let your unsurpassable might be the bridal price.

"In case you are wondering how can I, who dwell in the women's quarters in the inner palace, be carried away without the murder of my relatives, let me share something with you. In the morning, before the wedding, I will lead a procession of women to the temple of Girija, Parvati of the mountains, our Kula Devi, the Goddess of our family. Thus will I be outside the palace at this opportune time.

"If you fail to grace me by taking my hand, I shall give up my life by fasting unto death and other austerities. Not just in this lifetime, but in lifetime after lifetime shall I do so until I attain you as my husband.

"O, lord of the Yadavas! I have sent you this private message. Whatever is to be done has to be carefully thought out and done at once."

Thus the letter concluded. One can only marvel at the boldness, intelligence, confidence, and thoughtfulness of the princess who penned this message. In fact, there is a great lesson for us in sadhana and bhakti in this story.

On the one hand, it is true that Rukmini, as the embodiment of Lakshmi, and Krishna, as an avatara of Vishnu, were destined to be married. On the other hand, there is deep significance in the act of Rukmini writing this heart-

felt, unabashed letter to Krishna and taking the initiative in asking him to marry her.

We should have the same openness and sincerity towards Iswara as Rukmini demonstrated; the same conviction that if we simply ask Bhagavan to accept us, She/He must and will. Simply through hearing the glories of Krishna, she fell in love with him. Similarly, through listening to and reading the stories of Bhagavan's leela, we, too, can develop an intimate and close connection with our *ishta devata*, our chosen form of the Divine.

Krishna took the hand of the messenger and smiled.

"I, too, am always thinking of her, just as she is thinking of me. I am unable to sleep at night. I know that because of her brother's opposition, our marriage has been blocked. Defeating those corrupt kings in battle, I shall take away this beautiful girl, so absorbingly in love with me, just as fire is extracted out of the fire stick in a sacrifice."

Krishna ordered his charioteer, Daruka, to prepare his chariot. Then he ascended the chariot with the brahmana messenger. The four swift horses, Saibya, Sugriva, Megha-pushpa, and Valahaka, were harnessed to the chariot. They covered the distance to Vidarbha in one night.

When Balarama, Krishna's older brother, learned of Krishna's destination, he, too, departed for Vidarbha. He took with him a strong contingent of chariots, elephants, cavalry, and foot soldiers. He sensed a great battle brewing.

RUKMINI AWAITED the arrival of Krishna on the top floor of an observatory in the capital city. Hours passed as she watched over the empty roads being decorated for her upcoming nuptials. She worried that Krishna may have found her plea defective and was unwilling to marry her.

Her mind grew absorbed in despairing thoughts of Krishna, and she closed her tear-drenched eyes for some time. Suddenly, her left thigh, hand, and eye twitched, portending auspicious tidings. She opened her eyes with a smile and reminded herself that there was still time for Krishna to arrive.

At that moment, the brahmana messenger entered her inner apartments to report back to her. She rushed to meet him. Skilled as she was in divining people's thoughts from their external expressions, she began smiling before he could say a single word. She knew he bore good news.

The messenger informed her of the arrival of Krishna at the capital and of Krishna's vow to carry her off as his bride. Rukmini was so overjoyed that she fell at his feet wordlessly, unable to think of any gift she could give to the brahmana in recompense.

KUNDINA WAS the capital city of the kingdom of Vidarbha. In anticipation of Rukmini's marriage, the streets and squares of the city were swept and watered. Garlands and banners decked the walls and arches. The fragrance of burning frankincense wafted out from freshly dusted and cleaned houses. The people who thronged the streets were anointed with sandalwood paste and wore flower garlands and jewelry.

Krishna and Balarama soon arrived in Kundina. The citizens of Vidarbha were excited to see such distinguished beings in their midst. They chatted amongst themselves and a chorus of voices started to proclaim loudly that Rukmini alone deserved to be the wife of Krishna and that Krishna was the only befitting husband for Rukmini. The citizens all prayed that, if they had accumulated any spiritual merit in their lives, let those merits be dedicated to the feet of Bhagavan so that Krishna and Rukmini be allowed to wed each other.

∽

RUKMINI STARTED for the temple of Girija the next morning, accompanied by elderly female relatives and attendants as well as her girlfriends. Observing a vow of silence, she walked slowly and deliberately at the head of the procession, guarded on all sides by fully-armed soldiers. As she walked, the ground thundered with the blare of trumpets, the blasting of large drums, and the blowing of conches.

On reaching Girija's temple, Rukmini washed her hands and feet and entered the shrine with a calm mind. Several elderly brahmana women, conversant with the shastras, helped her worship Devi.

Rukmini prayed, "O Devi! I prostrate again and again before you and your sons, Ganesha and Skanda. May Krishna become my husband!"

Rukmini broke her vow of silence and came out of the temple, holding the hand of a lady-in-waiting, revealing her dainty fingers resplendent with gem-studded rings.

∽

POSSESSED OF A SLENDER WAIST, having a face reflecting the luster of her earrings, the charming Rukmini, wearing a gem-studded girdle around her waist, with budding breasts, a sweet smile, and restless eyes that darted this way and that under curly black tresses of hair, walked like a swan among the crowds of men who stared at her. Her teeth shone like white jasmine buds and her feet resembled tiny lotus buds.

Rukmini swept aside her hair and looked shyly amongst the kings for her beloved. The kings were so bewitched by her that they lost control over their weapons and collapsed in a faint in their chariots.

Rukmini and Krishna's eyes met. Seeing her eagerness to join him, Krishna carried her to his chariot. They ignored everyone else and took off in Krishna's chariot, accompanied by Balarama and others.

THE KINGS WERE INFURIATED at this kidnapping of the bride intended for Shishupala. The royal forces began raining volleys of arrows down upon Krishna's army. Rukmini watched as the skies darkened with the clouds of arrows that soon obscured Krishna's army from her sight.

Krishna saw the fear on her face and smiled at her in comfort.

"O, handsome girl! Do not be afraid. You will soon see our army destroy the army of our enemies."

Indeed, the fight raged on for some time. Eventually, most of the kings gave up. They could not withstand the attacks from the forces of Krishna and Balarama. Shishupala, the man to whom Rukmi had promised his sister, lay down his weapons, too. He looked so forlorn, standing by himself, staring at the woman he had lost that the other kings flocked to his side to comfort him.

Rukmi, the brother of Rukmini, was the last man standing. He jumped out of his chariot, sword in hand, and rushed at Krishna. It was as ineffectual as a moth flying into the fire. Krishna's arrows cut Rukmi's sword and shield into pieces. Krishna drew his sword to kill him.

Rukmini fell at Krishna's feet and begged him to spare her brother's life. She was in such agony that her limbs trembled and her golden necklace dropped to the ground. Out of consideration for her, Krishna stopped himself from killing Rukmi. As a compromise, he tonsured him instead.

Balarama, as any good brother-in-law should do, mediated between the couple in their first marital conflict. He took turns comforting Rukmini and scolding his younger brother.

Humiliated, Rukmi vowed to stay alone and away from the capital until Krishna was slain and his sister taken back. He built a new palace, Bhojakata, and stewed in his resentment and fury.

In the meantime, Krishna took Rukmini back to his kingdom of Dwaraka. Crowds of men and women from all over the land, hailing from the clans of the Kurus, Srinjayas, Kekayas, Vidarbhas, and Kuntis thronged the streets to see them. Everyone listened in awe as the minstrels sung about Krishna's abduction of Rukmini, which would indeed become one of the greatest love stories of all time.

～

NOTE:

It would be remiss, in a book on Hindu love stories, to not mention the eight forms of Hindu marriage.

The Manu Samhita describes eight principal forms of

Hindu marriage: Brahma, Daiva, Arsha, Prajapatya, Asura, Gandharva, Rakshasa, and Paisacha.

The Brahma form of marriage is the bestowing of a daughter upon one who is learned in the Vedas and of good character. This form of marriage is considered to be even more auspicious than divine marriage.

The Daiva form of marriage is a slight variation, in that the groom is a purohit or the officiating priest who is already conducting the sacrifice. The offering of the daughter takes place after the sacrifice has already begun.

The Arsha form of marriage occurs when the father bestows his daughter upon a husband in exchange for some cattle.

In the Prajapatya form of marriage, the couple comes together specifically for procreation and to raise children together. The father of the bride instructs the married couple, "May both of you be partners for performing religious and secular duties." In this case, the groom is usually the one who makes the proposal instead of the father.

The Asura form of marriage is where the groom gives away as much wealth as he can to the bride and the family of the bride in exchange for the marriage. Note that in none of these forms of marriage does dowry exist—the bride's family never gives money or wealth to the groom's family.

The Gandharva form of marriage is the union of a man and a woman by mutual consent. This is the closest to the modern notion of romantic love, premised on mutual desire and passion, but was never universally prescribed for all.

The Rakshasa form of marriage, which Rukmini urges Krishna to employ, is marriage by abduction or capture. This is referred to as the Rakshasa form, because the Rakshasas are known for cruelty and the use of violence. So, this kind of marriage is not generally encouraged.

Finally, there is the Paisacha form of marriage, which is not commended for anybody. This is when a man drugs a woman or takes her when she is asleep or unconscious. It is speculated that this vile form of marriage, which no one sanctifies, was only recognized as a way to give legal protection to the female who was violated.

Part Three

Sometimes Love is Fleeting

7

Menaka & Vishwamitra

I t would be impossible to discuss Hindu love stories without talking about Apsaras. The term *Apsara* is woefully translated in general as *nymph*. But Apsaras are so much more than that. They are female spirits of the clouds and waters, renowned for their exquisite dancing. They are beautiful and elegant, often the wives of the *Gandharvas*, another class of celestial beings who are acclaimed musicians. Some of the most famous apsaras are Urvashi, Menaka, Ramba, Tilottama, and Ghrtachi.

Often the Apsaras are sent at the behest of the Devas to interrupt the penance of ascetics. Why would the Devas want to break the meditation of sages and rishis? Well, the cosmic cycle of life, of birth followed by life followed by death, depends on the *yajna*, the sacrifices that are offered to discharge the karmic debts owed by man to the Devas, the rishis, the ancestors, humanity, and all sentient beings. This five-fold system of sacrifice is known as the *pancha mahayajna* (the five great sacrifices).

When a person intent on moksha—on escaping the

cycle of birth and death—sets his or her heart on transcending the world, the Devas get a little nervous. Who will feed them through sacrifice? The very order of the universe could be disturbed.

In fact, Vishwamitra, whose love affair with Menaka we'll be getting to momentarily, had so much *tapobala* (power of penance) that he was able to create an alternate universe. That universe was so close to reality that even today we have a whole class of vegetables known as Vishwamitra vegetables said to belong to that pseudo-reality, which some Hindus avoid eating.

So, the Devas will often test the rishis and other renunciates to see if they really, truly, most definitely do want to abandon the mortal world, to transcend the dualities of samsara, and attain that elusive effulgence known as Brahman. And if they do pass the test, then the Devas are delighted to have such an enlightened and attained one in their midst.

Many times, though, the Apsaras succeed and men who have lived in forests and caves for hundreds of years give in to their seductive charms. After the passion is spent, they realize that all of their tapobala has been drained and they must start all over again. The ups and downs of this spiritual life are metaphorically depicted in the popular children's game Snakes and Ladders, also known as Chutes and Ladders.

With that, let us start this story.

Vishwamitra had created his parallel universe and had even created another heaven. Indra, the king of the Devas, was frightened. Vishwamitra was a temperamental sage, and Indra did not want to face off with him in a fight. Better to cut him down to size before he could challenge Indra's throne and potentially usurp his position, he thought.

So, Indra turned to Menaka and asked her to help him. The Gandharvas and Apsaras are especially dear to Indra, as they regale his palace with their musical concerts and dances.

Indra pleaded with Menaka. "O Menaka, you are the first of the Apsaras. That Vishwamitra is like the sun in splendor, enraptured in contemplation. Any moment, he may toss me from my throne. Oh, do go and tempt him, my dear, frustrating his ambition. Win him away from meditation, you slender-waisted girl. Who but you, O, beautiful one, could attract him with your youth, agreeableness, mastery of the arts, smiles, and sweet speech?"

Menaka was dubious. She had grown immune to praise, heaped at her feet so often.

"This Vishwamitra has a really bad temper, as you well know. Even you are anxious at the thought of him. How then could I possibly face him without fear?"

She listed some of Vishwamitra's most infamous acts. There was the time he made the gentle rishi, Vasishta, witness the death of his own children. He had once created a raging river just so he could conveniently bathe in it before his practices. He had created a second world and many stars out of anger. He had created a heaven for the cursed Trishanku, that troublesome one whose cause he had adopted.

How was a simple Apsara like her, asked Menaka of Indra, to escape his anger and not be burned to a crisp by his wrath? He, who could burn the three worlds by his sheer radiance, he who with a stamp of his foot could cause an earthquake, he who could take Mount Meru and throw it a great distance, he who could . . . well, you get the idea.

Menaka was never one to back down from a good challenge, though. So, she gamely took on the assignment. She was clever and immediately began plotting how to protect herself and increase her chances of success. She told Indra that Marut, the Deva of the Wind, should be present when she approached the rishi to disrobe her in a flirtatious way. Kamadeva, the Deva of Desire / Love (who we will read about shortly), would also be needed, she informed Indra, to set the scene. It would also be nice, she said, if Indra could ask Marut to send along a fragrant wind to further entice the rishi.

Indra quickly acceded to each request. With a sigh, Menaka left the pearlescent skies of Amaravati, the capital city of Indra, and headed down to Earth.

MENAKA ARRIVED at the ashram of Vishwamitra. He was engrossed in penance. Sometimes he stood on one leg for hours. Sometimes he sat in the midst of the burning heat of five fires, under the scorching sun. In the morning, he stood in the cold river, muttering mantras all the while, again on one leg. She watched him in awe, impressed by his fierce countenance and unmatched determination.

A grumbling from the skies told her that Indra, who presided over thunder, clouds, and rain, was impatient. Menaka prostrated before Vishwamitra once and then began her work at a distance from him. She danced slowly, fluttering her hands in the scented breeze that Marut had sent, sending bursts of fragrance in the rishi's direction. She swayed this way and that until the wind Marut had sent caught her white upper cloth and lower cloth, stripping her. Menaka ran this way and that, trying to catch her wisps of clothing, careful to blush and appear bashful. She furrowed her brows in mock consternation with Marut, the Deva of the Wind.

Vishwamitra saw all this. At first, his eyes were cold and imperious, annoyed at this interloper. But when her body was revealed to his gaze, shorn of all clothing, he saw that her physique was flawless. He saw that there was no mark of age on her at all. He saw the grace with which she danced, the elegance with which her hips swayed. And he was overcome with lust.

He crooked his finger, indicating that he wanted her. She accepted with a smile. And then they passed a long time in each other's company. Years passed; many years passed, and it felt to them as if only a day had passed. They delighted in each other.

One day, the spell broke. Vishwamitra was saddened to realize that the accumulated balance of his tapobala had been depleted, that so many years of austerity and penance had been lost just like that. Dejected, he started anew on his quest to become a *Brahmarishi*, a member of the highest category of rishis.

In the meantime, Menaka had become pregnant. As the time of delivery approached, she went to the banks of the Malini River, which flowed along a valley among the beautiful mountains of the Himalayas. There, she gave birth to a daughter. She left her on the banks of the river and returned to Deva Loka, her mission on Earth completed.

We are not told in the Mahabharata what Menaka and Vishwamitra felt at the time of their separation. Were they reluctant to part? Or had it been nothing more than lust, as easily forgotten once it had passed as if it had never been at all?

That is left to our imagination, but that they genuinely did care for each other, that there was indeed a strong and irresistible attraction between the fiercest of rishis and the foremost of Apsaras is most probably true. It is said that they did meet once more, in a different place and a different time, when Vishwamitra was once again engaged in austerities. They spent another ten years together before Vishwamitra sent her away again.

That baby, that child of Vishwamitra and Menaka, abandoned on the banks of the river, was vulnerable in that forest abounding with lions and tigers. A group of vultures took pity on that baby and sat around her to protect her. Because she was protected (*tala*) by the vultures (*shakun*), she became known as Shakuntala. Her story, her journey from abandoned child to queen and queen mother, is one of the most cherished and hallowed tales in all of Hinduism and Indic literature.

Shakuntala gave birth to Bharata, who became a mighty emperor and founded the dynasty after whom the Mahabharata is named.

Kalidasa, one of the greatest poets and dramatists ever born, wrote a celebrated play named after Shakuntala. This was translated into English and German and became wildly popular in Europe.

In fact, Goethe once said:

> WOULD'ST thou the blossoms of spring,
>   as well as the fruits of the autumn,
> Would'st thou what charms and delights,
>   would'st thou what plenteously feeds,
> Would'st thou include both heaven and
>   earth in one designation,
> All that is needed is done, when I Sakóntala
>   name.[1]

One last word on Menaka. It is easy to look upon her as a heartless mother. But it would be unfair to measure the Apsaras and others by the standard of human morality. In Kalidasa's version of the story, in fact, she comes back to help her daughter when she is in trouble as a young woman and mother.

8

Pururavas & Urvashi

The story of Pururavas and Urvashi is one that dates back to the Ṛg Veda and is found in the tenth mandala. A separate prose version is also found in the Shatapatha Brahmana, with some variation. Later versions of the story appeared throughout the Puranas, and this episode was also featured in one of Kalidasa's plays. It is also a story of deep esoteric significance, symbolizing the intimate relationship between the Sun (represented by Pururavas) and the Dawn, or Usha, represented by Urvashi, an Apsara.

This love story that has enthralled Hindus from time immemorial is condensed into a single hymn in the Ṛg Veda. It starts with Pururavas chasing after Urvashi. He beseeches her to wait for him so that they can talk, insisting that they must talk this very day.

Urvashi is impervious to his pleas:

"What shall I do with this speech of yours? I have marched forth, like the foremost of the dawns.

Pururavas—go off home again. I am as hard to attain
as the wind."[1]

Then comes a most obscure verse that has been interpreted in different ways. In the Vedic hymn, Pururavas
decries that Urvashi, under the will of no man, is like an
arrow shot from the quiver of beauty, one who will keep
flashing forth like lightning, like the bleating of a lamb so are
her tempestuous outbursts displayed.

They bicker back and forth, Pururavas reminding her of
their happier times together, Urvashi chafing against his
pressure on her. She reminds him that they were together
once and she had given into his desires back then, hinting
that what was in the past should be left in the past:

"Pururavas, I followed your will. You were then the
king of my body, you hero."[2]

Pururavas persists. The cool Urvashi then reminds him
of his kingly duties in a subtle and sly way. She refers to their
son, and how the rivers and other Apsaras helped raise him,
just as how, for waging great battles, for smiting the enemies,
the Devas had created Pururavas. She chides him that he had
been born to protect others but was instead harassing her.

But Pururavas will not relent. When will his son come
to him, he asks. When will his son shed that tear, the
moment he finally recognizes him as his father, when will
that moment come? Who can keep apart a married couple?

Urvashi is as hard as nails. She tells him that she will

send him the child, that thing of his that is with her. She
tells him to go home for he will not attain her. She calls him
a fool.

Pururavas has grown dejected and tries to arouse her
pity. He says,

> *"And if the gods' pet should fly away today,*
> *never to return, to go to the most distant*
> *distance . . .*
> *Then he might lie in the lap of Dissolution.*
> *Then again the ravening wolves might*
> *eat him."*[3]

Even this threat of death does not move her. She tells
him not to die, not to fly away, not to let those wolves eat
him. She points out that there can be no lasting union with
women, for they have the hearts of hyenas. And yet there
appears to be a softening within her, too. She reminisces
that when she took the mortal form and spent four autumns
with him, once a day, she consumed a drop of ghee. From
that, she says, she continues to be sated even now.

Perhaps this is the lesson that she is imparting to him.
That, even if love is fleeting, just a little bit can be enough,
that we should not be greedy for more and more of that
which attracts us but rather learn to subsist on what little
has been allotted to us. There is a saying that love can exist
for a reason, a season, or a lifetime. Our mistake is that we
try to make last that which cannot last forever.

Pururavas begins to understand the futility of his quest.
He utters these eloquent lines:

> *"She who fills the midspace, who is the*
> *measurer of the dusky realm, Urvashi—I,*

> the best (of men?), seek to bring her
> under my sway.
> "Since the granting of a good deed will stand
> you in good stead, turn back: my heart is
> scorched."[4]

The hymn concludes in the voice of the Devas, bringing to an end this marital quarrel that is not so very different from the kind of bickering couples engage in even now. They tell the Aila king that the two of them will still be bonded until death. Their child will be a mortal who will make sacrifices to the Devas, but Pururavas is promised that he will one day rejoice in Swarga, the heavenly realm of the Devas.

This enigmatic and compelling narrative has manifested itself into different interpretations across Hindu literature. We learn more about Pururavas in the Puranas and the Mahabharata. He was born on Mount Puru, from which he derived his name. He was made king of the entire Earth. The Devas were his friends and even the Asuras were his followers.

According to the Mahabharata, Pururavas had gone to the region of the Gandharvas. There, he had met and fallen in love with Urvashi. He brought from that place the three kinds of sacrificial fire for mortals to employ on Earth. It is said that Urvashi bore him six sons: Ayus, Dhimat, Amavasu, Dhridhayus, Vanayus, and Satayus.

Another version of the story stems from the narration provided in the Shatapatha Brahmana. In this version, Pururavas and Urvashi fell in love with each other. He asked her to marry him, and she agreed with a few conditions. One, that Pururavas would protect Urvashi's pet sheep, and two, that she would never see him naked. Pururavas agreed, and they married.

Indra started missing Urvashi in his court, and he tried to find ways to break the conditions. He sent Gandharvas to kidnap the sheep when they were making love. Urvashi heard the cries of her pets and scolded Pururavas for breaking his word. He jumped up naked and ran after the sheep. Indra then produced a flash of lightning so that Urvashi saw him naked, thus breaking the other condition. This part of the story hearkens back to that esoteric verse from the Ṛg Vedic hymn but plays it out in a different way.

Urvashi then left Pururavas and returned to Swarga. Pururavas was heartbroken. She would still come to Earth occasionally and bear him children, but they were never completely reunited.

Part Four

Kama, Too, Must Be Honored

9

Agastya & Lopamudra

Entire books could be written about Agastya and likewise about Lopamudra. Both are incredible individuals who came together as one of the most revered and important couples in Hinduism. Their story first comes to us in the Ṛg Veda and is then elaborated upon further in the Mahabharata.

Lopamudra was a rishika. Several hymns from the Ṛg Veda have been attributed to her. To be a rishi or rishika means to "have seen" a mantra or hymn from the Vedas. The rishis do not compose or author the Vedas or anything in the Vedas; the Vedas are *apaureshaya*, or not of human origin. To the rishis and rishikas are the Vedas revealed, such that they "see" the mantras of the Vedas and become *mantra-drashta*, seers of the Vedas. Lopamudra is also acclaimed as a *mantradrika*, one who is well-versed in the mantras of the Ṛg Veda.

The name *Lopamudra* signifies the loss (*lopa*) that befell the animals and plants who gave up their distinctive attractive features to Agastya. Agastya then took all the best features of all the species to fashion into creation Lopamudra. After creating her, Agastya entrusted her to the King of Vidarbha's guardianship as the king was seeking a child. But Agastya had always intended to marry her.

Once she grew up, Agastya asked for her hand in marriage. Lopamudra agreed and left the palace for his hermitage.

Agastya was a devout rishi, always engaged in austerities and rites. Lopamudra soon felt lonely and neglected. One of the hymns in the Ṛg Veda carries verses where she seeks his attention and love. The hymn plays out as a dialogue between the couple, capped by an observation from a student.

In the hymn, Lopamudra laments:

> *For many autumns have I been laboring,*
> *   evening and morning, through the aging*
> *   dawns.*

> *Old age diminishes the beauty of bodies.*
> *   Bullish (men) should now come to their*
> *   wives.*[1]

Agastya is persuaded and they reignite their romance. The student admires at the end Agastya's devotion to both love and austerity. Eventually, they have a son together, named Dridhasyu, who grows up to be a poet.

THE MAHABHARATA further elaborates on this story. Yudhishthira had traveled to the ashram of Agastya. Lomasha Rishi then narrated to him the story of Agastya and Lopamudra. This is the tale he told.

Once, there was a city known as Manimati. There, a Daitya (son of Diti, one of the clans of Asuras) named Ilwala lived with his younger brother, Vatapi. Once Ilwala asked a brahmana to grant him a son equal in valor and prowess to Indra, the king of the Devas. The brahmana refused, and Ilwala was furious.

He developed a vicious plan of vengeance against the brahmanas he now hated. He transformed his younger brother into a ram. This was easy enough as Vatapi had the ability to assume any form at will. Then Vatapi in the form of that ram would be marinated and cooked, and finally offered to the brahmanas as food.

That's when the real mischief would begin.

For Ilwala had the power to summon to him any person or being. Even if that person had died and gone to the abode of Yama, the Deva of Death, he or she would be revived and sent back straight away to Ilwala if he called his or her name. So, every time the brahmanas ate, Ilwala would loudly utter Vatapi's name. And Vatapi would rip open the flanks of the brahmanas and come out with a laugh. In this way, many innocent brahmanas perished.

While this was going on, Agastya, an illustrious rishi, during his travels came across his deceased ancestors. They were hanging upside down above a pit. Surprised to see them in this state, Agastya asked them what had happened to them. They replied that they were waiting for their line to be continued, that they would remain in this state unless and until he fathered a son.

The Sanskrit word for *son* is *putra*, which means one who saves his parents and forefathers from the hellish realm known as Put. So, it was traditionally believed that by having sons who could carry out the sacrificial rites and offerings to the ancestors, one would have a smooth passing and afterlife.

Agastya wished to do well by his ancestors. He thought about having children. But he could not find anyone in the world who he could accept his wife, nor could he find anyone in whom he could take birth in the form of a son. Thus he took together the most beautiful parts of different creatures and melded them together into the form of a woman named Lopamudra. He gave her away to the king of Vidarbha. She grew, day by day, like a lotus in the midst of water or the effulgent flame that becomes a fire.

Her foster father was a wealthy ruler. She was surrounded by a hundred maidens and shone in their midst, just like Rohini outshone the fainter constellations in the night sky. Soon, Lopamudra exceeded even the Apsaras in beauty. She was so well-qualified in all dimensions that even when she reached maturity, no man dared to ask for her hand in marriage.

Just as the king was beginning to despair, Agastya Muni came back. He requested the king to bestow his daughter upon him. The king straight away fainted. Lopamudra had grown accustomed to the fineries of palace life—how could he banish her to the jungle in the company of an ascetic?

But the king dared not refuse. He approached his wife, the queen, and explained to her his dilemma. Her face grew pale in sorrow, but she, too, did not say a word. Lopamudra came to them and sought to relieve them of their concern. She asked her father to give her away to the rishi. And so they were wed.

Agastya Muni may have consented to marry and become a father but he was definitely planning on remaining a renunciate.

After their wedding, Agastya said to Lopamudra in that

brusque voice that new husbands sometimes use, "Cast away your costly robes and ornaments."

Lopamudra did so, giving away trunks full of clothes, and adopted a simple wardrobe of dresses made of bark and deerskin. She became as austere as her husband. The couple began to practice penance together. Agastya grew to love his wife as the two embarked on their journey together to perform rites, perceive the mysteries of the universe, and see and record profound Vedic hymns.

One day, after a long time had passed, Agastya saw his wife emerge from the river after her bath. It came over him all at once, an overwhelming feeling of affection for this woman, for her devotion, purity, and restraint, for her grace and beauty. He beckoned her, indicating that he wished to be with her.

Lopamudra folded her hands together in front of her chest and spoke sweetly to her husband.

"No doubt the husband marries his wife for the purpose of having offspring. But you, my husband, must reciprocate the love I have showered upon you. O regenerate one, you should arrange for me a bed like the one I had in my father's palace. Come to me adorned with flowers and ornaments, and I, too, will be decorated and ornamented in a pleasing away. How can I come before you in these rags? It is not a sin, after all, to dress up for such an occasion."

Agastya protested, "My blessed girl, you slender-waisted one, I do not have the wealth your father possesses."

"It cannot be that a great ascetic like you lacks the power to summon in an instant all that exists in the mortal world."

"Certainly, I can. But that would be an expenditure of my tapobala. My wife, ask for something that will not deplete my store of tapobala."

Lopamudra cast an appraising eye over her body and met his gaze.

"The time will soon pass. My season will not last long. I do not wish to consummate our marriage in any other way. Nor do I wish to diminish your ascetic merits. Thus you must find a way to do as I desire without depleting your tapobala."

Agastya Muni nodded. "So be it. I shall go pursue wealth. Stay here and wait for me."

Agastya then embarked on his quest. He had resolved that no matter what, he would not obtain wealth in a way that would bring harm to any creature. He approached multiple kings and explained to them that he wished for a portion of their wealth but only to the extent that it would be possible to take the money without injuring anyone. The kings shared with him the details of their revenue and expenses, and one by one, he rejected their offers of wealth. He understood that in each instance it would not be possible to take that money without causing harm to somebody else.

After several such futile visits, the kings came up with an idea. They suggested to Agastya that he go to the Asura king, Ilwala—remember, that wicked king who turned his brother into a ram and kept killing brahmanas by having his brother tear them apart from the inside? Yes, that one! Ilwala was inordinately wealthy. The kings offered to accompany Agastya on a visit to him.

Ilwala received them graciously enough with his fake hospitality. As was his habit, he transformed his brother into a ram and cooked the meat for the kings. All the others became demoralized and depressed looking upon that Asura in the guise of a chopped-up ram for them to eat. Agastya comforted them, promising that he would take care of matters. And he ate up the entire dish of meat, consuming every morsel of Vatapi.

After the dinner had ended, Ilwala summoned his brother. But instead of his brother tearing out the flesh of Agastya Muni from inside, nothing happened other than Agastya letting out a loud belch. Well, a very loud belch, actually, one that was as loud as the roar of thunder. Ilwala called out for his brother over and over again, but there was no response.

Agastya burst into laughter. "How can he come out? I have already digested him."

Ilwala groaned in despair, dropping his head into his hands. He realized the power of the great rishi and prostrated before him.

"Why have you come here, and what is it you want of me?" Ilwala's voice had become meek.

Agastya smiled at him. "We know you to be exceedingly wealthy. These other kings who have come with me do not have that much money, and I need a lot of money quickly. Give us what you can, without depriving anyone else."

Ilwala consented.

Agastya did some quick calculations. "Per my math, you must give to each of these kings ten thousand cows and an equivalent number of gold coins. For me, you must give twice as much as that, plus a gold chariot and some horses that are exceptionally fast, as swift as thought." He was in a hurry to get back to his wife, now that his mission was nearly accomplished.

Ilwala frowned.

Agastya Muni smiled. "Do not worry. If you ask, you will find out that your chariot has been turned into gold. That is the very chariot you may give away to me."

Ilwala found out that the rishi was indeed telling the

truth. With a regretful heart, the king gave away all that wealth that had been requested for the kings and for the rishi, plus the golden chariot, plus two special horses named Virava and Surava. Then, the kings and Agastya all left and went back to their respective homes.

Agastya decked out a bed and himself for his beloved wife.

Lopamudra was delighted. "You have fulfilled all of my wishes, O illustrious one. Now father a child upon me, one who will be full of great energy."

Agastya stroked her hair tenderly. "I am so pleased to have you as my wife. Tell me, wife, would you like to have one thousand sons, or one hundred sons each equal to ten sons, or ten sons each equal to one hundred, or just one son who may vanquish one thousand?"

Lopamudra immediately replied, "May we have one son equal to a thousand. One good and learned son is preferable to many worthless ones."

"So be it."

After she became pregnant, Agastya retired to the forest for a time. The baby grew in Lopamudra's womb for seven years. Finally Dridhasyu was born. Even as a child, he would carry large amounts of sacrificial materials into his father's ashram. Thus was he called Idhmavaha (the carrier of sacrificial wood).

10

Kamadeva & Rati

I t is not possible to write about Hindu love without paying homage to Kamadeva, the Deva of *kama*. *Kama* is a complex term that refers to a sense of enjoyment, including within the scope of that the fulfillment of desire and longing in a romantic sense. It would be a crass oversimplification to reduce this notion to 'love' in the sense that we use it nowadays.

In Hinduism, every human being is entitled and obligated to pursue the *Purushartha*, which are the four principal aims of human life—namely, dharma (the pursuit of that which is appropriate conduct for an individual in any given circumstance; an individual's dharma is in consonance with the larger principle of dharma that upholds the harmony and order of the cosmos as a whole for the sake of *loka sangraha* [the welfare of all sentient beings]); *artha* (the pursuit of wealth in accordance with dharma); kama (the pursuit of enjoyment in accordance with dharma); and, finally, moksha (self-realization and transcendence of the apparent cycle of birth and death).

It is said that Kamadeva was created from the mind of

Brahma. He was under instruction to facilitate procreation throughout the world by shooting his flower-tipped arrows to induce desire in others. Daksha Prajapati, the father of Sati, who became Shiva's wife, in turn, was requested to present a wife for Kamadeva.

Kamadeva first used his arrows against Brahma and the Prajapatis, who were also charged with creation. Their eyes fell upon Sandhya, the Devi of Twilight, embodying all the beauty and enticement of dusk and dawn. She was Brahma's daughter, but even Brahma himself grew infatuated with her through the power of Kamadeva's arrows.

At this moment, Shiva happened to pass by. He saw what happened, shook his head in disgust, and laughed. Brahma and the Prajapatis trembled and perspired in fear. Shiva had a most fierce temper, and no one wanted to face him in his fury. From the sweat of Daksha Prajapati emerged the beautiful Rati. Daksha Prajapati presented her to Kamadeva as a suitable bride for him.

Rati derives from the Sanskrit word *rama*, which can loosely be understood as one who brings joy. Thus, for example, the name of Rama, one of the most beloved avatara of Vishnu, signifies that he brings enjoyment to others. Kamadeva and Rati grew into a couple deeply in love and traveled the three worlds together.

Kamadeva is an ever-young Deva wielding his sugar-cane bow, strung with honeybees. The flowers on his arrows are imbued with five different kinds of fragrance to please each of the five senses: ashoka tree flowers, lotus flowers, blue lily flowers, jasmine flowers, and mango flowers. The ashoka tree flowers represent fertility; the lotus purity in life; the blue lily represents peace; the jasmine induces seduction; and the mango flowers bring prosperity and satisfaction.

Always at Kamadeva's side is his green parrot. And the makara, a crocodile or sea creature, adorns his banner. Parrots are known to be affectionate toward each other and are also monogamous, so this choice of vahana is indeed appropriate for Kamadeva. Rati carries a discus and lotus, and she remains unparalleled in desirability.

Another version of the story starts with Rati as a not particularly attractive Devi. No one noticed her or wanted to marry her. Lakshmi, the wife of Vishnu, was moved by her plight. Lakshmi taught Rati how to apply the *solah shringara*, or the sixteen classical adornments for a woman. Who better than Lakshmi to teach this to Rati, as the *shri* in *shringara* refers to auspiciousness and is another name for Lakshmi herself?

The sixteen adornments are the bindi (the sacred dot of kumkum or vermillion powder applied at the spot of the third, mystical eye), *sindhoor* (applying vermillion powder at the parting of the hair); the *maang tikka* (a hair accessory that is worn at the parting of the hair); *kajal* (kohl used to line the eyelids in smoky black—traditionally, this was made from the soot of an oil or ghee lamp); a nose ring; earrings; a necklace; designs of henna; bangles; an armlet worn on the upper arm; eight finger rings to be worn on all the fingers except the thumbs; a hair accessory with gold or flowers; a decorative waist belt; anklets; toe rings; and fragrance.

Applying the solah shringara made Rati the most beautiful woman in the three worlds. Kamadeva fell in love with her immediately, and they became the happiest of couples.

That would not last, though, because of Shiva. It was almost inevitable from the start that the Deva of Kama would clash with Shiva, the Adi Yogi, the most renunciate Mahadeva. From the very beginning, from the first arrows Kamadeva ever shot, his destiny had become linked with

Shiva's. Long after the time that Shiva had laughed at what Kamadeva had done to Brahma and the Prajapatis, fate brought them together again.

Shiva had lost his wife Sati and had withdrawn from the world. The Devas needed him to reengage with the world and reunite with Parvati—who was none other than Sati reborn—for a variety of reasons. First and foremost, his withdrawal from the cosmic order was hastening Pralaya, the dissolution phase of the cycle of creation and destruction. That was not good for anybody. Second, there was a powerful Asura, Tarakasura, who was pestering the Devas. The son of Shiva was fated to slay him, so they need to rouse Shiva and get him to father a child. (This is the child who eventually grows to become Skanda, who we read about earlier.)

The Devas summoned Kamadeva and charged him with the task of helping Parvati seduce Shiva. He was reluctant to anger the great God. He had seen his friends, the Apsaras, suffer from terrible curses because they had interrupted the penance of rishis. How much worse would Shiva's temper be, he who had been born as Rudra, howling with fury into the world as he came into it? Poor Kamadeva was not as powerful as the other Devas, though, and had no choice but to take on the challenge.

With a sigh, he went to Shiva's side. Shiva was oblivious to his presence, lost in meditation as he was. Kamadeva and Rati did their usual work, creating a springlike atmosphere with beautiful flowers and a scented breeze. Kamadeva trembled as he shot his arrows at Shiva. His aim was both successful and fatal—successful at rousing Shiva and afflicting his heart, fatal to himself as Shiva opened his third eye and burned poor Kamadeva into ashes.

At the same time, Shiva's gaze had fallen upon Parvati

and his heart was stirred. He asked her in a gentle voice to ask of him any boon.

The ever-compassionate Parvati consoled Rati, devastated at the incineration of her husband. Parvati, who had spent so many years undergoing penance and austerities to win over Shiva, could easily have asked for Shiva to marry her. But her kindness and compassion compelled her to ask Shiva to restore Kamadeva to life.

Shiva agreed, both out of affection for Parvati and also because he had calmed down by then. But actions cannot simply be undone. So, for some time, Kamadeva had to exist in a formless fashion and was thus known as Ananga, one without any limbs. But in time, promised Shiva, he would indeed be reborn. With that, Shiva slipped into meditation once more.

∼

MANY THOUSANDS OF YEARS PASSED. Eventually, Kamadeva was reborn as Pradyumna, the son of Krishna and Rukmini (you may recall their story from earlier). When Pradyumna was but six days old, he was kidnapped by Sambara, a frightful Asura.

The meddlesome Narada Muni had informed Sambara that Pradyumna was destined to kill him, and so Sambara was intent on killing him first. Sambara threw the baby into the cold waters of the vast sea and went back to his home.

A large fish swallowed the baby, and then that fish was caught by fishermen and delivered to Sambara's home for dinner. Mayadevi, the mistress of the household, oversaw the workings of the kitchen. When the fish was cut open, she saw the beautiful child inside. As she froze in shock, Narada Muni once again appeared and explained to her the situation. He counseled her to care for this jewel of mankind.

Narada Muni likes to create trouble, as he did when he told Sambara about the one who would kill him, but he also is the one who helps resolve the crises he sets into motion. It is through these challenges that many auspicious things happen.

Mayadevi was in fact none other than Rati reborn. She had come to the mortal world to help protect her husband from the cruelty of Sambara. She raised him and guarded him from Sambara. As he grew into his teenage years, she imparted to him all her teachings on magic and the arts.

One day, Pradyumna grew suspicious of the strange affections of Mayadevi.

"Why do you treat me in a way that does not appear to be purely maternal?"

She replied, "You are not my son. You are the son of Vishnu. Sambara kidnapped you and tried to kill you, but I rescued you. Your mother is somewhere else, weeping for you."

When Pradyumna realized the truth of the matter, he was enraged and challenged Sambara to battle. After finally killing Sambara and his forces, Pradyumna flew to his parents' palace and landed with Mayadevi there. There was a happy family reunion.

Narada came to wrap up the loose ends, explaining that Mayadevi was never Sambara's wife but had only appeared in that household to protect Kamadeva, her real husband, from harm.

The story of Kamadeva teaches us that love is important. Even Shiva, the greatest of all ascetics, welcomes and accepts the love of Sati and then Parvati. It is the appearance of Kamadeva and his work that saves the world from hurtling into doom, even as Kamadeva was bereft of his body for a long time to come as a result.

Kamadeva and Rati are also responsible for inspiring seminal texts on love, romance, and sensuality within the Hindu tradition. From their dialogues spring forth profound discourses on these topics, just the way the dialogues between Shiva and Parvati have resulted in sacred texts on Hindu metaphysics and philosophy.

Part Five

Devotion

11

Usha & Aniruddha

We have read the story of Pradyumna, the son of Krishna, and Kamadeva reborn. Now, let us read a perhaps even more romantic story about his son and the grandson of Krishna and Rukmini, Aniruddha.

Aniruddha's first marriage was to Rochana, the daughter of Rukmi, the brother of Rukmini. Rukmi, you may remember, had opposed his sister's marriage to Krishna, had been humiliated and defeated in battle, and had vowed lifelong enmity with Krishna. To make a long story short, the occasion of his daughter's marriage to the grandson of Krishna did not go well and Rukmi ended up getting killed by Balarama, the elder brother of Krishna.

Perhaps that is making it too short. What had happened was, after the wedding ceremony, some kings instigated Rukmi to challenge Balarama, Krishna's older brother, to a game of dice.

It was said that Balarama was not particularly good at gambling, although he enjoyed it. So, the first three matches were lost by him to Rukmi. As the king of Kalinga laughed at him, Balarama bristled in irritation.

The next game was won by Balarama, but Rukmi proclaimed himself to be the winner. By now, Balarama was furious. He challenged Rukmi to another match, but Rukmi falsely claimed victory again.

A voice announced from the sky that Balarama had won fair and square, and that Rukmi was lying.

Rukmi did not concede. He ridiculed Balarama in front of all of the other kings present:

"You fellows are mere cowherds and forest dwellers. Only kings of royal dynasties know how to play at dice and fight with arrows, not men like you."[1]

Unable to bear this insult, Balarama struck Rukmi down with his club and killed him. He knocked out the teeth of the king of Kalinga too, for good measure.

Krishna kept silent, as he did not want to upset either his wife or his brother during this rather awkward situation.

Then, Krishna placed Aniruddha and Aniruddha's new bride on a beautiful chariot and headed back to Dwaraka.

As if that were not enough marital drama, Aniruddha's second marriage resulted in a war between Vishnu and Shiva.

∽

IT STARTED WITH BANASURA, an Asura who was the son of Bali. Asuras are not always totally bad, you know. Banasura, for example, was devoted to Shiva, noble in character, intelligent, and honest. He ruled the kingdom of Sonitapura. Having won Shiva's favor, even the Devas were deferential to him.

Banasura had one thousand hands. This delighted Shiva, as Banasura was able to play so many percussion instruments at once as Shiva danced his dance of destruction, the Tandava. Pleased with the Asura's devotion, Shiva had given him the boon that Shiva himself would guard his palace.

Usha was Banasura's daughter. One night, she dreamt of Aniruddha, even though she had never seen him or even heard of him. That dream was so powerful that she fell in love with him right then and there.

When she woke up, she was desperate to find him. Her friend, Chitralekha, offered to help. She asked Usha to describe the literal man of her dreams in exact detail and promised to bring him to her, if he existed.

Usha described a male figure whose eyes were lotuslike, who was dark blue in complexion with powerful arms, dressed in yellow robes.

Chitralekha tried to puzzle out who it could be. As the daughter of a prominent minister, she had encountered many different men, including male Devas, Gandharvas, Yakshas, and other classes of celestial beings. She started drawing portraits of prominent male figures, anyone she could think of. When she drew Pradyumna's body, Usha became shy, taking him as her father-in-law.

Chitralekha smiled slyly and began to draw a sketch of Aniruddha. Usha bent her head toward the drawing and proclaimed that he was indeed the one.

Chitralekha was a no-nonsense kind of girl. She immediately took off to fetch and bring Aniruddha to her friend's side. It helped that she had yogic powers and could fly. In a moment, she flew off to Dwaraka.

Aniruddha was sleeping. Chitralekha picked him up, careful not to awaken him, and flew him back to Sonitapura. She took him directly to Usha's bedchamber, which was otherwise inaccessible to men.

Usha's delight knew no bounds. She pampered the prince with sandal paste, the finest food and drink, incense, and elegant clothing. Aniruddha, when he awoke, was equally smitten with Usha. They spent hours in conversation and companionship. They lost track of time, so immersed they were in enjoying each other.

Usha soon became pregnant.

Soon, the guards had an inkling of what was going on. They reported to the king that she did not appear to be a maiden anymore.

Banasura immediately marched into his daughter's quarters. His jaw fell open at the sight that greeted his eyes. There was his daughter playing dice with a young man who wore on his chest a garland of jasmine flowers, tinted crimson from the saffron powder that decorated Usha's breasts.

Aniruddha was used to battle. He rose to his feet and lifted his metallic mace, ready to strike anyone who dared to interrupt his time with his beloved Usha. He quickly broke the bones of Banasura's soldiers, and those guards ran away from the palace.

Banasura, infuriated, tied up Aniruddha, ignoring the protesting wails of his daughter.

~

IN THE MEANTIME, in Dwaraka, the entire palace was disconsolate at the disappearance of their beloved prince. The four months of the rainy season had passed without any sign of his whereabouts.

Narada, who could never stay in one place for more than a moment and therefore got all the good news and gossip hopping from place to place, came to Dwaraka. He informed Krishna and the others of what had happened to Aniruddha and that he was now besieged in Sonitapura.

Krishna, Pradyumna, and all the Vrishni forces set out for Banasura's kingdom, intent on bringing back their prince. Banasura in the meantime gathered an equally large army to face the forces of Dwaraka.

Then ensued a great battle when the two armies met. Shiva, prone as he was to give away boons more generously than prudent, was now bound to defend Banasura. Krishna and Shiva faced off against each other, and Pradyumna (the son of Krishna) confronted Skanda (the son of Shiva). They shot missiles at each other, counteracting one with another —a wind missile being defeated by a mountain missile, a fire missile being destroyed by a water missile, and so forth.

Eventually, Krishna dispatched a missile that caused yawning and sleepiness. This dazed Shiva and struck down many soldiers on Banasura's side.

Seeing his armies cut down like this, Banasura was wrathful. He ran to fight Krishna himself. Taking advantage of his thousand hands, Banasura strung five hundred bows together and shot two arrows from each of them.

Krishna cut all the bows of Banasura in an instant and also destroyed the charioteer, the chariot, and the horses of Banasura. Krishna lifted his conch shell and sounded it, a low roar that spread over the battlefield.

Banasura's mother was watching from the sidelines,

nervous about what would happen to her son. She chewed on her lip and then came up with an idea. She ran onto the battlefield, ignoring the shouts of protests from the soldiers and her son.

She stripped off her clothes and stood before Krishna naked with her hair tousled and disheveled. Krishna turned away. This gave Banasura the chance to retreat and retreat he did.

In the meantime, Shiva had revived. He sent the Saivaj-vara, the fever of Shiva, to fight Krishna. The fever was three-headed, three-legged, and hot, threatening to burn everything in its wake. Krishna conjured up his own fever, which was cold, as befits the one who reclines in the milky waters of the Ksheera Sagara. The two fevers fought each other.

Finally, Shiva's fever was forced to retreat and fall at the feet of Krishna. The fever of Shiva began to praise Krishna, seeking refuge. Krishna blessed the fever of Shiva, as he blesses anyone who seeks to take shelter at his feet.

Banasura could not resist and came back to the battle-field to take one other shot at Krishna. Krishna calmly proceeded to cut the asura's hands off, one by one.

Shiva, who can never bear to see his devotees in pain, approached Krishna and asked him to show mercy to Bana-sura as he had done before for other Asuras.

Krishna readily agreed.

"Whatever is dear to your heart, I shall do accord-ingly. And whatever you have decided I accept."[2]

Krishna also promised that the four arms left remaining

to Banasura would never age and that he would have no cause for fear.

Now that everyone was happily reconciled, Krishna led his family back home, placing Aniruddha and Usha at the front of the procession.

12

Chyavana & Sukanya

Anyone who has dabbled in Ayurveda would be familiar with the powerful health tonic known as *chyavanprash*, a thick jam combining several different herbs and other ingredients. This concoction is named after a great rishi from the Vedic times, whose wife helped restore his youth and vitality with this tonic.

The story of Chyavana Rishi first comes to us from the Shatapatha Brahmana. He belonged to the Bhrigu dynasty, who were themselves the descendants of Angirasas. Once, while the Bhrigus were away, Chyavana was alone in the ashram. He was senile and old.

King Saryati, a son of Manu, was hunting in the forest surrounding the ashram. The rishi was immersed in meditation. He had been meditating for so long that white ants had covered his body. Only his eyes were visible. The king's hunting party mocked Chyavana, and he cursed them. The curse sowed a rift within the king's family. When the king understood the source of the trouble, he offered his daughter up as a bride to the rishi.

After some time, one day, the celestial twins, the

Ashwins, had come to the ashram and tried to seduce Sukanya, the daughter of the king, she who had married Chyavana Rishi and cared for him. Sukanya rejected their advances, which was no mean feat considering that the Ashwins are considered to be the most handsome and attractive of the Devas.

Sukanya instead asked them to restore Chyavana's youth. The Ashwins are always up to a good medicinal challenge. They are associated with medicine, health, science, and the dawn.

They subjected the rishi to three treatments. Certain herbs were immersed into a pond, and they asked Chyavana Rishi to bathe there. They applied an herbal paste to his body. And then they prepared another herbal paste, that which we even today consume as chyavanprash, for him to ingest. This process of rejuvenation is one of the most ancient and powerful systems of healing and nourishment, of restoring good health, known as *Kayakalpa*.

The treatment worked and Chyavana was indeed transformed into a young, healthy man. Delighted, Sukanya suggested that the Ashwins be entitled to a share of the sacrificial offerings made in Kurukshetra, effectively promoting their status to full-fledged Devas.

THE MAHABHARATA HAS an elaborated version of this story. An origin story is also provided on how Chyavana got his name, which means to have fallen. Once, Puloma was being pursued both by Bhrigu, the rishi, and a demon. She was pregnant with Bhrigu's child. The demon came to Bhrigu's ashram and asked Agni, who was watching over Puloma, whether Bhrigu had married Puloma yet according to the proper rites. Agni said, no, that they had not been married like that.

The demon, seeing his opportunity, took the form of a hog and carried away Puloma. Puloma was in the advanced stages of pregnancy and the distress of the abduction resulted in the premature birth of the baby boy, who fell to the ground. He was thus named Chyavana. He was so radiant that at his appearance the demon burnt to ashes.

Puloma then carried the child back to the ashram, waiting for Bhrigu to arrive. She was so distraught that she wept enough tears to form a river, known as Vadhusara. When Bhrigu returned and found out what happened, he cursed Agni to become one who eats anything and everything.

THE STORY of Chyavana Rishi's marriage to Sukanya is elaborated upon in the Mahabharata and some of the Puranas. Chyavana Rishi was immersed in meditation and covered in a mound of white ants. He looked no different than a heap of earth.

One day, King Saryati came to visit the serene lake where the rishi was meditating. He came with four thousand females and also his only daughter, named Sukanya. Sukanya was enchanted by the beautiful scenery of the lakeside and the neighboring forest.

She was in a romantic mood and intent on frolicking. She began to walk among the trees, plucking flowers from the blossom-laden branches. Chyavana watched her wandering across the forest floor, unchaperoned by her maids, wearing only one skimpy dress. The old rishi desired her and called out to her.

But she did not hear him.

After some time, Sukanya noticed the ant hill. She mistook the rishi's eyes for worms and poked at them. Chyavana was in excruciating pain, but, perhaps charmed as he was by Sukanya, he did not curse her.

Nevertheless, the dire consequences of his wrath were felt throughout the kingdom. The soldiers of King Saryati's army were not able to — relieve themselves from the calls of nature. In other words, they could neither urinate nor defecate. The condition spread across the kingdom and started to infect animals also.

The king was alarmed and investigated the matter. Sukanya by this time realized what had happened and confessed to her father that she had mistakenly stabbed the rishi's eyes. The king dashed to the rishi's side to beg for forgiveness on behalf of his daughter.

Chyavana Rishi, angry though he was, could not forget the beauty of Sukanya or his desire, which had been inflamed after so long. He told the king that the matter could be resolved if the king would allow him to marry Sukanya.

The king panicked. The rishi was old and now blind, and King Saryati could not imagine giving away his cherished daughter to such a man. He returned to the palace dejected. Sukanya approached her father and told him she was willing and ready to marry the rishi. The king sorrowfully led her to the forest and left her with Chyavana.

Sukanya and Chyavana began a contented life together. She cared for him, practiced austerities alongside him, looked after guests in their ashram, and tended the sacrificial fire.

One day, the Ashwin twins happened to see Sukanya

right after her bath while she was still naked. They were immediately smitten and introduced themselves to her.

Right away, Sukanya informed them that she was married to Chyavana. They were shocked and indignant on her behalf. He was old and ugly, practically senile. How could such a pretty, sweet girl be wasted on such a man, they wondered.

It is worth taking a moment to appreciate the poetic lyricism of the Mahabharata in K.M. Ganguli's prose translation, the first in English of the unabridged Mahabharata. Here is his translation of the Ashwins' speech to Sukanya:

"What for, O fortunate one, hath thy father bestowed thee on a person who is verging on death? Surely, O timid girl, thou shinest in this wood like lightning. Not in the regions of the celestials themselves, O girl, have our eyes lighted on thy like. O damsel, unadorned and without gay robes as thou art, thou beautifiest this wood exceedingly. Still, O thou of faultless limbs, thou canst not look so beautiful, when (as at present) thou art soiled with mud and dirt, as thou couldst, if decked with every ornament and wearing gorgeous apparel. Why, O excellent girl in such plight servest thou a decrepit old husband, and one that hath become incapable of realising pleasure and also of maintaining thee, O thou of luminous smiles? O divinely beautiful damsel, do thou, forsaking Chyavana accept one of us for husband. It behoveth thee not to spend thy youth fruitlessly."[1]

Sukanya arched an eyebrow at them.

"I am devoted to my husband. Do not question or doubt my faithfulness."

The divine twins were reluctant to give up on her. They came up with another plan. They furnished their credentials as celestial physicians and promised to restore youth and grace to her husband. Then, she would have to choose one among the three of them to be her husband.

Sukanya was reluctant to do this, unwilling to take any gamble that could cause her to be taken away from her husband. But when she consulted with her husband, Chyavana was eager to consent. Perhaps he wished to become a more virile and handsome husband for his wife's sake.

In any case, Chyavana quickly entered the water. The Ashwin twins joined him. In the next moment, all three males emerged from the water. The appearance of each male was gorgeous and identical, each of them wearing golden earrings.

In unison, the three males asked Sukanya to choose her husband from among the three of them.

She was confounded by the identical forms that each of them bore. She deliberated over it. It is said in the Devi Bhagavatam that she prayed to Devi for help. And then in the next moment, she picked out Chyavana from the three of them and took him as her husband once more.

The rishi was ecstatic at this turn of events. He desired to reward the Ashwin twins and promised that they would become entitled to partake of the soma in the presence of Indra himself. The Ashwins were delighted to hear this and went back to Deva Loka. Sukanya and Chyavana also lived together as a happy couple, just as if they were Devas too.

In time, King Saryati heard that happy news, and Chyavana offered to officiate a rite on behalf of the king in celebration. The king was overjoyed. At the rite, Chyavana portioned out some of the soma juice to be offered to the Ashwins. Just as he was lifting the ladle to make the offering, Indra appeared and put out his hand to stop him.

"The Ashwins are but physicians to the Devas," said Indra. "They have no entitlement to the offerings we receive."

Chyavana Rishi protested this inequity. How could the ones who had transformed him into an immortal youth, how could ones of such power not themselves be considered Devas?

"O lord of the celestials," Chyavana addressed Indra. "O destroyer of enemy cities! Let it be known that the Ashwins are also Devas!"

Indra scoffed and refused to let the sacrifice proceed. Their debate grew heated.

Chyavana again took up the ladle to complete the offering of the soma to the Ashwins.

Indra threatened him: "If you try, you will face my *vajra*." This was the thunderbolt weapon of Indra, one of the most powerful weapons in the universe.

Chyavana merely smiled and completed the offering. As Indra moved to hurl the vajra at the rishi, his arm became paralyzed by Chyavana. Chyavana recited hymns and finished the rites.

Then, he turned to Indra. Through his tapobala, Chyavana manifested Mada, a demon that was strong and gigantic. One of his jaws rested on the earth and the other stretched to the heavens. It appeared that he could and would swallow up the entire world.

Even the battle-hardened Indra licked his lips in fear at the sight of that demon rushing toward him while he remained paralyzed, each of his limbs rendered stiff and immobile by the rishi.

Indra sighed. He knew enough to know when he had been defeated; this was not the first time a rishi had gotten the better of him.

Indra called out, "Indeed, these two Ashwins will have a right to drink the soma offerings. I have resisted only to spread your fame, to show off your powers. Let it be as you wish."

He was used to making these eloquent pleas with minimal apology, as Indra had the habit of often angering the rishis.

Mada was destroyed, and Chyavana spent his days happily in the company of his loving wife.

Part Six

Rising, Not Falling

Note

Nowadays, it is customary to say that one has "fallen" in love. We associate romance with how desperate one is for the affections or the company of another. We measure 'love' by the extremity of passion, desperation, pathetic longing, and trauma we are willing to suffer just to obtain the company of another. The more obsessed, enthralled, and attached we are, the better.

In modern times, romance is perhaps best symbolized by something like King Edward of Great Britain abdicating the throne to marry Wallis Simpson. Whereas in Hinduism, the abiding standard of love and devotion is the story of Rama and Sita, where Rama gives up his beloved wife for the sake of his dharma as a king.

We have explored earlier the concept of Purushartha, the four principal aims of life. Dharma is always the first of the Purusharthas, because artha (the pursuit of wealth) and kama (the pursuit of enjoyment) must always be pursued in accordance with and subject to dharma.

The stories in this section are focused on couples who help each other rise through love rather than fall.

13

Satyabhama & Krishna

W e have read about the marriage of Krishna and Rukmini, his first wife. Krishna has more than sixteen thousand wives (yes, sixteen thousand). The Ashtabharya are his eight principal queens. According to the Srimad Bhagavata, these eight queens are Rukmini, Satyabhama, Jambavati, Kalindi, Mitravinda, Nagnajiti, Bhadra, and Lakshmana. While the sacred texts vary on some of the names of these eight queens, all acknowledge that, after Rukmini, Satyabhama has the second place of honor among Krishna's wives.

It is time for us to meet this spirited queen, who is considered to be a manifestation of Bhu Devi, or the Earth Goddess. Rukmini, on the other hand, is a manifestation of Sri Devi.

Satyabhama was the daughter of Satrajit. Satrajit had obtained the Syamantaka Jewel from Surya Deva, the God of the Sun, and refused to give it to Krishna once when he asked for it.

One day, Satrajit's brother, Prasena, who had apparently borrowed the ring from his brother, went hunting.

Unfortunately, he was killed by a lion. Jambavan, the King of the Bears, who lived in a nearby cave came across the carcass of Prasena. Jambavan killed the lion and gave the jewel to his daughter, Jambavati.

In the meantime, Satrajit discovered what happened to his brother and was crazed with grief. He surmised with no evidence that Krishna had killed his brother and stolen the gem. He began to spread these malicious rumors throughout the kingdom of Dwaraka.

Krishna was determined to prove his innocence. He set out to find the Syamantaka Jewel and finally traced it to the cave of Jambavan. He discovered the jewel tied around the neck of Jambavati.

When Krishna asked to take back the jewel so he could clear his name, Jambavan refused. Jambavan was loathe to part with what he considered to be his precious jewel.

And so Krishna and Jambavan fought each other for twenty-eight days. Jambavan grew weak from the sword cuts inflicted on him by Krishna. Finally, he realized that Krishna was none other than Vishnu, whom Jambavan had served when he had appeared as Rama in his previous incarnation.

Jambavan grew remorseful. He returned the jewel to Krishna and offered his daughter, Jambavati, as a bride for Krishna. Krishna returned the Syamantaka Jewel to Satrajit, who apologized to him for all of the trouble he had caused.

Satrajit was riddled with guilt. He wondered how he could possibly recompense Krishna for the unfounded slander. He realized there was nothing more precious that he owned than Satyabhama, his daughter, and the Syamantaka Jewel. He offered both to Krishna.

Krishna agreed to the marriage but refused the jewel.

He said slyly to Satrajit—

"We shall not accept the jewel Syamantaka. It is best that it is with you who are a devotee of the Sun-deity. We too may afterwards benefit by it (as Satyabhama is your only child to inherit your possessions)."[1]

ONE OF THE most important incidents related to Krishna and Satyabhama is the slaying of Narakasura. Brahma had granted this troublesome Asura a boon that he would die only when his mother wished him to die.

This emboldened Narakasura to be a cruel tyrant who oppressed his people. He was particularly well known for his disrespect toward Devas and women. What mother will wish for her son to die? He was not going to be easy to destroy.

Over time, Narakasura defeated even Indra and abducted sixteen thousand women, whom he kept in his palace. He had brazenly stolen the earrings of Aditi, the mother of the Devas. This proved too much for Indra. He requested that Krishna kill Narakasura and liberate the worlds from the terror of his reign. Krishna agreed to his request. After all, Indra was the older brother of Vishnu, and Krishna was an avatara of Vishnu.

Krishna took off for Narakasura's capital city, accompanied by Garuda, his eagle vahana, and his beloved wife, Satyabhama. A particularly beautiful version of this incident is narrated in the southern rescission of the Hari-vamsha, which is a supplemental section of the Mahabharata. (While often referred to as an appendix to the Mahabharata, the Harivamsha is a gigantic text in its own right. A ten-volume hardcover version takes up half of a shelf in my bookcase. It is a sacred text in its own right.)

For a long time, the battle raged on between Krishna and Narakasura. Narakasura cunningly aimed at Garuda, the eagle-mount of Krishna, wounding him badly. Blood started spurting out of every pore of Garuda's body right in front of Krishna's eyes.

In pain and anger, Garuda began flapping his wings over and over again. He swiped at the Asura with his beating wings. Narakasura, in turn, started raining powerful blows upon the great bird's body. Then, he took an iron arrow and shot it at Krishna. The long and sharp weapon struck Krishna on the forehead, and Krishna sank into a swoon on the floor of his chariot.

Satyabhama was distraught to see her husband in this state. She began fanning him, trying to relieve his distress. Garuda, too, even in the midst of his frenzied pain fanned Krishna with his wounded wings.

Krishna revived and handed over his bow, named Sarnga, to Satyabhama. That weapon was so heavy that it could only be used in battle with great difficulty, even when wielded by experienced warriors.

Krishna told his wife, "Devi, you must now fight with Narakasura. I am too tired."

Satyabhama hardly needed encouragement. Her eyes were sparking with rage at this demonic being who had dared to strike at her husband. She lifted Sarnga and began to fight with Narakasura. She shot him with crescent-shaped arrows. She tormented him with arrows the way truth torments liars.

Narakasura's lips curled in disgust. He attacked her between her breasts with sharp arrows. He shot at her torso six fast-flying arrows and seven more arrows at her sides. In fury, Satyabhama broke his bow. She wielded her husband's weapon expertly, chopping into pieces the Asura's flag and flagpole, his umbrella, his chariot, and his horses. When Narakasura bent to pick up another bow, Satyabhama chopped that one into two also. Every time he picked up a bow, Satyabhama immediately broke each one into pieces.

Krishna rested against the back of Garuda and watched his wife admiringly.

Narakasura hurled a mace at her, and that, too, she broke. When he tried again, she laughed aloud. She pierced his body with sharp arrows.

Krishna stirred and began praising his dear wife, as did all the Devas and rishis, standing in the skies and watching her in awe.

While Satyabhama normally quite relished being flattered, she remained focused on the fight this time. She aimed arrows at the head of Narakasura's charioteer and, with a clean shot, decapitated him.

Krishna, overcome with delight, embraced her and tenderly wiped off the sweat from her body. He paused the battle to give her a necklace that she had long desired. It was the necklace that he, in his earlier avatara as Vamana Deva, had taken from Bali during Bali's sacrifice.

Satyabhama happily tied the necklace around her neck, becoming herself radiant with its luster. So many times she had begged for this necklace, while playing with Krishna and while she was in bed with him. He had always refused in the past. It delighted her more than any other gift.

Krishna said, "Beautiful Devi, rest now. You must be tired."

He picked up the bow and reengaged Narakasura in battle. Narakasura shot eight arrows at Krishna, ten at

Satyabhama, twenty-five at Garuda and then again seven more at Krishna. Now Krishna was starting to get angry.

Krishna broke Narakasura's chariot and killed his new charioteer. Narakasura jumped down from his chariot and approached Krishna on foot, hitting him with his mace. Krishna broke the mace. Then Narakasura began lifting boulders and throwing them at Krishna, who broke them all into pieces with his arrows.

Narakasura began to grow desperate. He fought with whatever weapon he could find—more boulders, trees, nooses, maces, slingshots, swords, axes, barbed missiles, lances. Krishna had enough and decided to finally kill the Asura. He brought out the Sudarshana Chakra, that serrated discus of gold that whirred above his finger, the fastest-moving weapon in the universe.

He released the chakra, aiming it at Narakasura's heart. In a moment, the heart of the Asura was cleaved in two and he died.

And what of the boon given to Bhu Devi that her son would die only when she wished it? Well, as it happens, Satyabhama was the incarnation of Bhu Devi, and therefore once Bhu Devi wished her son dead it so happened, fulfilling the terms of the boon.

Krishna then took back the stolen earrings of Aditi and restored them to the mother of the Devas. Aditi gifted the earrings to Satyabhama, touched by her devotion to Krishna. She also blessed Satyabhama that she would stay young and beautiful forever.

Even today, the victory over Narakasura is celebrated as Naraka-Chaturdashi, the night before Deepavali/Diwali. Krishna then rescued the sixteen thousand women who had been held captive by Narakasura. He consented to marry them to protect their honor.

In other versions of the story, such as is found in the Srimad Bhagavata, it is only Krishna who slays Narakasura but the version narrated above has become a popular conceptualization of the tale and is commonly depicted in paintings and other artwork related to the episode. Satyabhama has always been admired as a spirited, courageous woman who fights alongside her husband on the battlefield.

14

Hemachuda & Hemalekha

Tripura Rahasya was considered by Bhagavan Sri Ramana Maharishi as one of the greatest works to expound on Advaita Vedanta. Vedanta is one of the six *darshanas* (philosophical systems) of Hinduism. Vedanta, literally the end or essence of the Vedas, emerges from the foundation of a trio of sacred texts, namely, the Upanishads, the Brahma Sutras, and the Bhagavad Gita — this group of texts is also referred to as the *prasthanatraya*.

Within Vedanta, there is Dvaita, Vishishtadvaita, and Advaita which have varying ontological and metaphysical premises derived from different interpretations of the prasthanatraya. Advaita, which literally means one-without-a-second, is a system of non-dualism, best captured by its interpretations of Upanishadic statements like *tat tvam asi* (That Thou art), *ayam atma brahma* (this Self is the Brahman, the Whole).

Tripura Rahasya expounds upon Advaita Vedanta through a series of parables and teachings delivered by Dattatreya to Parashurama. One of the fascinating aspects of this profound text is that embedded in it is the story of a woman who acts as guru to her husband, leading him from ignorance to enlightenment.

Parasharuma, an avatara of Vishnu, was a fierce brahmana. He had scourged Bharat, the traditional name for India, twenty-one times, killing all the kshatriyas, the members of the ruling and warring class, he could find, including babies. Twenty-one times he purged and exterminated the kshatriyas. He would get overcome by rage each time and keep repeating the cycle.

Even his ancestors urged him to stop. He took it to heart but then fell into a fresh fury when he heard about the appearance of Rama, another avatara of Vishnu. He could not accept that he was not able to suppress the might of kshatriyas from rising again. Parashurama then challenged Rama to a fight and lost.

On his way back from that battle, mortified by defeat, Parashurama realized that there must be more to life than this. He wanted now to understand the truth of all things, the unchanging and undying truth, the one reality that underpinned it all. He therefore approached Dattatreya for guidance.

Dattatreya is one of the most revered gurus and masters of yoga in all of Hinduism. He is considered to be an avatara of the Trimurti—Brahma, Vishnu, and Shiva. The Tripura Rahasya takes place as a dialogue between Dattatreya and Parashurama.

Dattatreya assured Parashurama:

"Just as a man sinking in the ocean suddenly finds a boat to rescue him, so also your virtuous actions of the past have now placed you on the most sacred

heights of self-realization. That Devi Tripura, who
is the conscious core of the heart and therefore
knows each one intimately, swiftly rescues her
unswerving devotees from the jaws of death, after
manifesting Herself in their hearts."[1]

DATTATREYA BEGAN HIS INSTRUCTION. He told the story
of Hemachuda, one of two sons of Muktachuda, the king of
Dasarna. Once, Hemachuda and his brother, Manichuda,
led a hunting party into a forest in the Sahya Mountains
infested with tigers, lions, and other beasts. They hunted
many deer, lions, boars, bison, wolves, and other creatures.

As more and more wild animals were killed, a tornado
began to rise. Sand and pebbles poured down over the
forest. Dust screened the sky, rendering it dark as night.
The hunting party grew frightened. Some hid under rocks,
others in caves, and some behind trees. The two princes
rode away in different directions.

Hemachuda reached an ashram in the midst of a lovely
garden. There he saw a young woman who shone like gold.
He was besotted with her at first sight. The woman was
poised and gracious. She welcomed the prince and told him
to tie his horse to the tree and take rest. She plied him with
fruit and juice.

The woman explained that this was the ashram of the
sage Vyaghrapada, a devotee of Shiva. Her name was
Hemalekha, and she was the sage's foster child. Once, an
Apsara had come to bathe in the river bordering the ashram.
The king of Vanga had come at the same time and they fell
in love. She became pregnant and tried to abort the fetus,

but Hemalekha was born alive. Later that evening, the sage Vyaghrapada came to the riverbank for his evening bath. Seeing the baby, he picked her up and raised her with a mother's love.

Hemalekha said, "He who offers righteous protection is said to be the father. I am therefore his daughter by virtue of this and devoted to him."

She then instructed him to await her foster father's return.

Hemachuda was charmed by Hemalekha, but he grew anxious at the thought of meeting her father. Hemalekha smiled; his thoughts were known to her. She counseled him to be steady and forthright, to tell her father all that he wished to say.

At that moment, Vyaghrapada returned, carrying a basket of forest flowers for worship. The prince prostrated before him, introducing himself, and took his seat as directed by Vyaghrapada. He was too tongue-tied to express his desire to marry the sage's daughter.

The sage, however, understood the situation in one glance. The prince's face was lovelorn. Desiring the best for his daughter, Vyaghrapada meditated upon what would be the appropriate course of action. He decided to consent to the marriage between Hemalekha and Hemachuda.

Hemachuda was overjoyed, as was his father when he heard the news.

THE COUPLE WAS married and honeymooned in the palace, in forests, and in other scenic spots. But Hemachuda noticed that his wife was not as romantically inclined as he was. In fact, he thought she was downright non-responsive.

One day, he asked her, "Why is it that you are not as attentive to me as I am to you? Why do you never seek pleasure with me? Even during our most passionate moments, you appear to be indifferent. How can I be happy if being with me does not bring you enjoyment? Even when I listen to your every heartbeat, your mind appears to be elsewhere. When I speak to you, it is as if you are not even listening."

Hemalekha heard the words of her infatuated husband, who was always holding her to his chest. She looked at him closely and decided that perhaps the time had come for her to teach him a few things. She smiled at him and spoke to him tenderly.

"O Prince, it is not that I do not love you. I am trying to discover the truth of what is the greatest joy in life, which will never become distasteful. I am always searching for it but have not found it. What do you think it may be?"

Hemachuda laughed derisively. "Women are indeed silly. Do not even the birds and beasts, even the crawling insects, know what is good and what is bad? That which is pleasing is clearly good and that which is not is bad."

Hemalekha kept her voice neutral. "Indeed you are right that women are silly and cannot understand such things. So you, the one of righteous discernment, must teach me. Then I will stop thinking in this way and will be able to share in your pleasures just as you wish."

Hemachuda opened his mouth to keep speaking, but Hemalekha continued.

"You say that happiness and misery result from what is or is not pleasing. Yet, do we not find that the same object yields pain or pleasure based on the situation? How then can your statement be the absolute truth? For example, the effect of fire depends on the season, the location, the size, and intensity of the flame. It can be a life saver or a killer; it can be pleasant in the winter or torturous in the summer. The same can be said of cold, of wealth, of sons, of one's wife, of the kingdom.

"When I think about it, no one seems to possess enough of anything to provide for lasting happiness. That which will one day provide misery, on account of being insufficient to provide happiness any longer, cannot be said to be a source of happiness. The satisfaction from the fulfillment of a desire before another desire takes its place cannot be said to be happiness, since the seeds of future pain are still latent."

Hemachuda was nonplussed.

But Hemalekha was not done yet.

"Even your perception of my beauty is nothing but a reflection of the conditioning of your mind. Beauty is nothing but a subjective mental concept. Just think, whatever pleasure you derive from my beauty, this is exceeded in other cases by others in their love or attraction toward their husband or wife, be they fair or ugly. The fair woman that you see in me is only the reflection of a subjective concept already embedded in your mind."

She extended this even further to make a statement about pluralism and diversity, in a way that we would appreciate today:

"The form, the stature, and the complexion of people differ in different countries and at different times. Their ears may be long; their faces distorted; their teeth large; their nose prominent; bodies hirsute or smooth, their hair red, black, or golden, light or thick, smooth or curly; their complexion fair, dark, coppery, yellow or gray. All of them derive the same kind of pleasure as you, Prince!"[2]

Overwhelmed by this torrent of words from his normally reticent wife, Hemachuda thought about all that she said. He was amazed by the thoughts she had expressed. He felt within him a disgust for worldly pleasures. Again and again, he discussed these points with his wife, trying to better understand the truth of what she was saying. He became pensive and withdrawn.

SOME TIME PASSED LIKE THIS. But Hemachuda was struggling. Neither was he able to enjoy life as he had in the past nor was he able to calmly detach. He thought about confiding in his wife about this, but pride restrained his tongue.

Inevitably, he began indulging once more in his old habits, glutting himself on fine food, wearing rich clothing and jewels, watching the dance of lovely women in his court —but every moment, his wife's words haunted him. He felt shame and self-disgust. He became pale and melancholic.

Hemalekha, who was attuned to each and every one of her husband's mood changes, went to his bedchamber and inquired after him.

"Why are you not as cheerful as before? What has made you sad?"

Hemachuda breathed a sigh of relief. He had been keener to unburden himself to his wife than he realized.

"How can I find happiness? Just as a man under order to be executed cannot enjoy the luxuries provided to him in his final days, so also I cannot enjoy anything. You tell me how I can become happy."

Hemalekha was pleased. She was eager to reveal the truth of her wisdom to her husband, but she had to pace herself to match his somewhat slower speed of learning. She presented to him a complex and elaborate parable, using as a metaphor an elaborate construct of a city, a queen, a friend of the queen, and so forth. She told him that this was the story of her own life. We do not have the space here to go through the parable in detail, but I highly recommend reading the entirety of the text of the Tripura Rahasya to delve into one of the most profound mystical and metaphysical treatises ever composed.

Hemachuda in his ignorance laughed at his wife.

"My dear, your words are frivolous and fanciful. What you have said is totally meaningless."

He reached out to playfully tousle her hair.

"Indeed you are the daughter of an Apsara. You are still young, hardly even a woman, but your long-winded speech is as if you are an old woman. Of what cities do you speak? Who is this friend of yours that you describe? My dear, I do not think that you are in your right mind."

Hemalekha was irritated. "How can you say that my parable is meaningless? Words from the mouth of one like me can never be nonsense. Do you think that I, your wife, would deceive you with a myth when you are sincere? Distrust of a well-wisher's words will inevitably lead to ruin. Mutual distrust will destroy all relationships."

She then discoursed on the importance of faith.

Hemachuda listened to her carefully but still had his doubts.

He said, "If faith should be had in anyone, my dear, it should certainly be placed in one who is worthy of it. One should never trust an incompetent person. Faith can only be put in the worthy, not the unworthy. I can therefore believe you only after fully ascertaining your worth, not otherwise."

Hemalekha smiled. "And how is it, husband, that one is to be judged to determine whether she is good or bad? Is the one who devised the standards for such measurement qualified to make such judgments? The judge's competence must be considered too. My husband, there is no end to such arguments. Life moves by faith only. People will not gain anything through endless discussion or blind acceptance. Of the two, though, there is at least hope for the latter but none for the former."

She then shared an anecdote to illustrate her point.

Hemachuda was astonished.

He exclaimed, "My dear, I did not realize how wise you are! Blessed am I indeed that I have fallen into your company."

Hemachuda felt peaceful and with renewed vigor he worshiped Devi with intense devotion. A few months passed like this, Hemachuda's mind absorbed in the quest for Truth.

ONE DAY, Hemachuda sought out his wife alone. Before, he had been reluctant to open up to her but now he had gained the humility to seek her out on his own.

Hemalekha received him into her chambers, offering him a seat.

She greeted him warmly. "Are you keeping well, my husband? I am seeing you after such a long time. Not a day passed by before without our meeting. How have you been spending your time? How do you spend your nights?" She embraced him tightly.

Hemachuda smiled. "My dear wife, you can no longer deceive me. I know the strength of your psyche and that nothing can disturb your equanimity. You are a sage indeed. I have come to ask your advice. Please explain to me that parable you described to me last time as the story of your life.

"Who is your mother? Who is your friend? Who is her husband? Who are her sons? What relationship do they have with me? I no longer believe this is a lie. I am sure you told me a parable full of significance. Please tell me everything in full so that I may understand it clearly. I bow to you with reverence."

Hemalekha was delighted. She gauged that he had indeed cultivated real dispassion to the vicissitudes of life and had also strengthened his mind and psyche. The time had come for him to be enlightened. She explained to him the meaning of the parable.

Hemachuda choked up once he understood the significance of her teachings. He asked questions to further clarify his understanding.

Hemalekha instructed her husband, "Listen carefully to what I am going to say. This is a subtle matter. Investigate the nature of the Self. Keep the intellect transparently clear. The Self is not an object to be perceived or described. How shall I tell you of it?"

Hemachuda did not say a further word. He rose from his seat, mounted his horse, and galloped away from the city. He rode to a royal lodge beyond the outskirts of the city. The crystal palace was beautifully decorated. He dismissed all the servants and ordered the guards to not

allow anyone to enter the palace while he was inside
without his permission, even if the king himself appeared.

HEMACHUDA CLIMBED up to the ninth story of the
building which looked out in all directions. He sat down on
a soft cushion. He then asked the guard to ask Hemalekha
to come to him. Within an hour-and-a-half, she was
climbing the steps of the palace like a celestial queen of the
night moving across the sky.

She found the prince, her husband, in perfect tranquil-
ity. She sat by his side and nestled close to him. He opened
his eyes, and she embraced him.

She asked him sweetly, "What can I do for Your High-
ness? I hope you are well. Please tell me why you have
asked me to come to this place."

He explained to her that he had done as she instructed,
retired to a solitary place where he could investigate the
Self. But he was having different visions and experiences
while trying to investigate the Self.

He had then forcibly restrained his thoughts, in an
effort to prevent the interference of mental activities. At
this, light had appeared, he had fallen unconscious, and
finally a feeling of bliss had overcome him for some time.
Was that light the Self, or was it something different?

Hemalekha, the knower of this world and beyond,
listened to him carefully. She nodded in understanding. She
explained to him that he had successfully repressed his
thoughts and turned his mind inward, which was a good
beginning. But that experience itself did not constitute self-
realization. Self-realization could not be subject to the
vagaries of an experience, since an experience was finite

and subject to beginning and end but self-realization was permanent.

Hemachuda nodded and resumed his investigation of the Self. He remained peaceful for a long time, unaware of anything beside the Self.

He awoke ninety minutes later and saw his wife. He closed his eyes again. Hemalekha took his hands and asked him to explain what he thought he gained by closing his eyes, or what he lost by opening them.

His lips trembled as if he were in a drunken state.

"I have found pure untainted happiness. I cannot find the least satisfaction in the activities of the world anymore. Enough! My dear, I beg you—let me fall again into that state of peace. I pity you that although you know this state you are not always immersed in it."

The wise Hemalekha smiled at this.

"My husband, you have not yet realized the highest state which is not tainted by duality. Once realized, the wise ones transcend duality and are never again confused. That state is still as far from you as the sky is from the earth. Your wisdom is no good, as it remains conditioned by closing or opening your eyes. Self-realization cannot depend on activity or effort."

Her speech clarified Hemachuda's confusion once and for all. The entire episode that takes place within the crystal palace is itself a mystical and yogic metaphor, full of esoteric meaning and significance. The text of Tripura Rahasya can and must be read at many different levels of cognition.

∼

GRADUALLY, Hemachuda became established in self-realization. Always steady in equanimity, he lived happily with Hemalekha and successfully reigned over his kingdom. He did all the things a king should do, without disturbing his self-realization. He made his kingdom prosperous; he engaged his enemies in war and won battles; he studied the scriptural texts of the shastras and taught them to others. He performed sacrifices and lived for a long time.

When his father, King Muktachuda, heard that Hemachuda had become a jivanmukta (one who has attained moksha while living), he consulted with his other son, Manichuda. They had known him best before he had met Hemalekha. They agreed that he had changed for the better such that he was no longer affected by pleasure or sorrow, treated friend and foe alike, and engaged in royal duties like an actor in a play, even while he always bore an otherworldly look. They sought him out and asked for the reason behind this change.

They, too, felt the desire to become jivanmuktas like Hemachuda. Even the ministers in the kingdom desired to be as tranquil and content as their crown prince. The queen, too, sought the same thing and was instructed accordingly by Hemalekha, her daughter-in-law.

In fact, all the citizens, all the artisans and members of all classes of people within the kingdom sought that state and were instructed by Hemachuda.

Even very young children and very old people were no longer subject to passion or the fear of death. The kingdom still carried on and everyone performed their duties, acting like actors in a drama like the rest of *Srishti*, creation.

What made this kingdom unique was that all the actions of daily life were done with full knowledge and wisdom; everything was done dharmically. A mother would rock the cradle with lullabies expositing high metaphysics. Dramatists entertained the subjects with plays depicting the truth of self-realization. Musicians sang only of wisdom. The entire state consisted of only sages and philosophers, whether they were men or women, servants or royalty.

Even the parrots and cockatoos in their cages parroted words of wisdom, the *mahavakya*, or the great statements, of Vedanta. They would say things like:

Meditate, O Man, on the Self, the Absolute Consciousness devoid of objects! There is naught else to know besides pure consciousness; it is like a self-luminous mirror reflecting objects within.

That same consciousness is also the objects, that is the subject, and that is all—the mobile and the immobile; all else shines in its reflected light; it shines of itself.

Therefore, O Man, throw off delusion! Think of that consciousness which is alone, illuminating all and pervading all. Be of clear vision.

Or:

Consider the Self as pure intelligence bereft of objective knowledge.[3]

Even the rishis called the kingdom the City of Wisdom when they visited it.

Dattatreya concluded, "By association with Hemalekha,

all people gained jnana (wisdom). Know then, that *satsanga* (association with the wise) is alone the root cause of self-realization."

That satsanga can take the form of a loving relationship between a husband and a wife, like in the case of Hemachuda and Hemalekha.

15

Chaitanya Mahaprabhu &
Vishnupriya Devi

I n Hinduism, there are two paths—one known as *pravrtti*, the path of world-affirmation and leading a conventional householder life, and the other known as *nivrtti*, the path of the renunciate who turns away from the external world. One is not better or worse than the other. Even those on the path of pravrtti can attain moksha in this lifetime, by living like a lotus in the mud of samsara without becoming tainted by it.

We find in the case of many great acharyas or spiritual masters that they come to a turning point in their lives, when they turn away from house and hearth, from the warmth and comfort of a family, to travel the path of nivrtti.

Sometimes, a woman, a wife, is caught in the middle. In the case of Sri Ramakrishna, who was wed to Sarada Devi, Sarada Devi, a *Sadhvi*, or saintly women, in her own right, eschewed the idea of a conventional marriage when asked by her husband. She wished instead to serve the religious mission founded by Sri Ramakrishna. She became the spiritual mother for the movement.

Other times, it may be genuinely difficult for a loving

wife to be left behind in her husband's spiritual quest. The poignant story of Vishnupriya Devi, the wife of Sri Chaitanya Mahaprabhu, epitomizes how this bittersweet grief and longing can transcend into the most powerful form of devotion that blesses both the lover and the beloved.

Sri Chaitanya Mahaprabhu lived in the 15th century. He founded Gaudiya Vaishnavism, which has grown into one of the most prominent *sampradaya* and *parampara* (sects and lineages) within the Hindu fold. He popularized *kirtan*, transforming *japa* (repetitive chanting of divine names) into a congregational exercise where people come together and sing the holy names together ecstatically, sometimes dancing madly in the streets, temples, and homes. Through kirtan and singing the names of his beloved Krishna, Sri Chaitanya Mahaprabhu spearheaded a resurgence of bhakti among the people of India.

His first wife had passed away at a young age. Sri Chaitanya Mahaprabhu was then around seventeen or eighteen years old and had become a renowned pandit. His mother, Shachi Mata, began looking for another wife for her son.

She consulted Kashinath Pandit, a well-known matchmaker in the area. Some consider Kashinath Pandit to be a reincarnation of the *purohit* (priest) sent by Satrajit, the father of Satyabhama, to arrange the marriage between Krishna and Satyabhama. Some consider Vishnupriya Devi to be a manifestation of Satyabhama as Sri Chaitanya Mahaprabhu is considered to be a manifestation of Krishna.

Kashinath Pandit then arranged the marriage between Sri Chaitanya Mahaprabhu and Vishnupriya Devi. Even as a child, Vishnupriya Devi was an intensely devoted girl. She would bathe in the Ganga three times a day. Shachi Mata had seen her at that time and always blessed her. Since she already knew the good qualities of Vishnupriya

Devi, Shachi Mata readily agreed to the proposed marriage. An auspicious date and time were then fixed.

Sri Chaitanya Mahaprabhu, golden in complexion, arrived at her father's house in a palanquin at dusk. They were wed according to the Vedic tradition and local customs. The next day, Vishnupriya Devi returned with him to his house. As she was crossing the threshold of her new home, she stubbed her toe on the doorway. She bit her lip to keep from crying out. She feared that this was a bad omen.

Sri Chaitanya Mahaprabhu pressed his toe on her injured toe to soothe it and gazed intently into her eyes for a moment. The touch of his feet removed her pain and his eyes removed all her fear. Contented, Vishnupriya Devi steadied herself and entered the household.

Since she was still young, she went back to her parents' house to be raised until she reached maturity. In the meantime, Mahaprabhu traveled to Gaya and received initiation from Sri Ishwar Puri. When he returned to Navadvipa, his birthplace where his mother and wife lived, he had become a transformed man. He was always crying out for Krishna and weeping with longing for him. He would be lost in meditation and ecstatic kirtan for hours, days at a time. All he could think about was Krishna.

Speculation started spreading that he would soon take *sannyasa*. Taking sannyasa means that one renounces one's past and one's connections with family and home, even one's name.

Shachi Mata fainted when she heard the rumor. She was too afraid to even ask her son whether the rumors were true. When she finally mustered the courage to broach the topic, Mahaprabhu confirmed that he was indeed intending to become a renunciate.

She cried out pitifully, "After the death of your father, after your elder brother took sannyasa, I have survived only by looking at your face. If you leave me too, I will certainly die."

Mahaprabhu listened with a bowed head. To comfort her, he told her the truth of his mission in life, the reality of her own nature and identity. He told her that in birth after birth, she had always been his mother and they were never truly separated, nor would they ever be truly separated.

By this time, Vishnupriya Devi had grown older and was now living with Shachi Mata and Mahaprabhu. But he hardly ever spoke to her. After initiation, he was always singing and dancing or lost in meditation upon Krishna.

On the day that Mahaprabhu finally decided to take sannyasa, Vishnupriya Devi had gone to the Ganga for her bath as was her custom. On the way, once more she stubbed her toe. Her toe started bleeding. In the middle of her bath, the nose ring that she had received on her wedding day fell into the Ganga. The nose ring is considered to be auspicious for a wife and is one of the sixteen adornments, solah shringara, that is traditional for a woman to wear.

Try as she might, she was not able to find and retrieve the ring. She wept bitterly all the way back home. Her mother-in-law asked her in concern what was wrong. Vishnupriya Devi explained what had happened. Shachi Mata comforted her, but she was inconsolable.

That night, Mahaprabhu entered Vishnupriya Devi's room in the evening. He seemingly never paid attention to her, so she was stunned to see him and did not know how to react. With love and tenderness, he decorated her, adorning her hair, placing a garland of flowers around her neck. He placed betel nuts in her mouth. For a long time, he conversed with her, his voice soft and textured with affection.

Vishnupriya Devi was riddled with anxiety. She thought to herself—

"A hurricane light burns brightly just when it is about to be extinguished. I see now that my fate may be like this."[1]

She sat and massaged his feet, tears flowing from her eyes.

Mahaprabhu opened his eyes when he felt the sting of her salty tears fall upon his feet.

He wiped her tears away. "Devi, you are beloved to me. Why is it that you weep?"

She wept uncontrollably. He asked her again and again what was wrong, but she would not say a word. She simply held his feet in her hands and wept. He pulled her up into his lap and cradled her against his chest, soothing her with murmurs.

After she had calmed, Vishnupriya Devi spoke. "My life, my beauty, my youth, my devotion, my dress and ornaments—they are all only for you. If you leave me, what will I do with my life? I'll be nothing more than a worthless pile of ashes."

He embraced her.

"Your name is Vishnupriya, she who is dear to Vishnu. Make your name true. Do not worry about the world. Devote your mind and body to Vishnu."

He could see she was still not convinced. He then

promised her that anytime she thought of him, he would appear in front of her. He gave his word.

Vishnupriya Devi temporarily forgot her pain. He joked with her, teased her, and satisfied her. Thus they spent their only and last night together.

Mahaprabhu did not want her to bear the pain of seeing him leave. Even though she was reluctant to sleep, through the power of yoga, he saw to it that she fell asleep. He glanced at her once, then stood up and walked out of the room.

After finishing his morning rites, Mahaprabhu touched his mother's feet. She sat like a statue at the doorway, eyes wide open but paralyzed with grief. And then he left Navadvipa and crossed the Ganga.

VISHNUPRIYA DEVI COULD NOT BEAR the agony of being separated from Mahaprabhu. She could not even eat food or drink water. Sensing this, Mahaprabhu appeared to her in a dream. He told her to have a deity of him carved from the wood of the magosa tree under which Shachi Mata had suckled him. In that form, he would always be with her.

Following his instructions, she had the deity made, the first of many deities consecrated of Mahaprabhu. Just as Rama had arranged for the construction of a golden statue of Sita after their separation rather than marry a second time, so also did Vishnupriya Devi tide over the pain of separation through the worship of Mahaprabhu in that deity. That deity is still worshipped to this day in Navadvipa. (It is one of the most powerful and beautiful deities I have ever seen.)

Vishnupriya Devi led a simple and ascetic life from

then onward. She only left the house once a day, to accompany her mother-in-law to the river for their daily bath. Only her feet were visible to others. No one even heard her voice.

She spent the entire day in front of that deity. In solitude, she would chant the mantra given to the world by Sri Chaitanya Mahaprabhu. After each utterance of the mantra, she would place a single grain of rice aside. After her chanting practice, which lasted most of the day, she would cook whatever rice had been collected like this, serve it to Shachi Mata, and then eat whatever little remained for herself.

Sri Bhaktivinoda Thakur shares the following pastime in his text, *Sri Navadvipa-Dhama-Mahatmya*.[2] Once, when Rama was in exile in the forest, he and Sita traveled through Navadvipa, in what is now West Bengal. Rama was observing the forest there and then smiled. Sita asked him why he was smiling.

Rama replied that in Kali Yuga he would be born in Navadvipa as Sri Chaitanya Mahaprabhu and she would be born as Vishnupriya Devi. In his youth, he would take sannyasa and his mother would weep, holding her daughter-in-law, Vishnupriya, in her arms. He told Sita that she would be that Vishnupriya Devi and he would thereafter remain in Puri and also weep for her day and night.

Vishnupriya Devi inspired many people. Before he took sannyasa, Mahaprabhu had faced significant local opposition. As people saw her devotion and austerity, the purity of her heart, and her unshakeable faith in Mahaprabhu, their enmity toward Mahaprabhu melted away and that *rasa*, that *bhava*, that mode of love-through-separation, which is the cornerstone of Gaudiya Vaishnavism, was made real and tangible by her.

16

Bilvamangala Thakur &
Chintamani

There is a *shubhashita*, a Sanskrit aphorism, literally a beneficial or auspicious saying, that instructs us never to examine the origins of a rishi, a woman, or a river. The idea is that it is less important what or who one once was than what he or she becomes, especially in the case of a rishi or a woman, who are societally expected to be beyond reproach. The paths to enlightenment are many and diverse.

There was once a renowned Vaishnava sadhu named Bilvamangala Thakur. He authored great hymns and literary compositions, full of devotion to Krishna. The story of his past life and how he rediscovered Krishna in his current life is a fascinating one. And he owed it all to a princess who became a prostitute.

It is said that in his past life, Bilvamangala Thakur was a great sannyasi and devotee of Krishna. He had intense love for Krishna. He would organize Srimad Bhagavata *kathas* (festive rites dedicated to reciting and teaching the sacred text). He would then personally feed *prasadam* (sanctified food offerings) to all those who had attended.

While organizing one of the kathas, he ran out of money to prepare the proper amount of prasadam. So, he went out to try to scrounge up some money. On the way, he came across a cremation ground where the body of a young princess was being prepared for burning.

Her father lit the fire, and then everyone left. The sannyasi looked at her corpse, weighted down with many jewels and golden adornments. He could not help but think that it would be useless to waste all this jewelry. It would be of no use to her corpse, after all, he reasoned. He thought it would be better for him to sell the jewelry and use the proceeds to prepare prasadam in large quantities.

When he reached for the ornaments, the voice of the dead princess rang out:

"Stop! If you need wealth, then go to the king. Tell him I have sent you. Under my bed there is a box full of treasure. Use that to serve Krishna and the devotees."

The sadhu did as she told. The king found the treasure and gave it to him. The sadhu expended all of the money he had received on the festival, but again, by the end, he ran out of money. In desperation, he went back to the cremation grounds. He took the diamond necklace from her body.

As he was leaving, the voice of the dead princess rang out again:

"You are committing a great wrong by stealing this necklace from me. That which is stolen can never be offered to the Gods. I curse you to take birth one more time and live an immoral life."

The sadhu did not return the necklace. One can become addicted even to performing meritorious deeds.

~

THE SADHU BECAME a womanizer in his next life. The princess also reincarnated as a prostitute with whom he fell in love, named Chintamani. He became obsessed with Chintamani.

After his father died, he waited not a moment after performing the death rites before running to her home. He had to cross a river to reach her side. A thunderstorm and roiling waves could not stop him. He held onto a corpse so as not to drown. When he reached the gate of her house and found it locked, he immediately climbed the wall, using a cobra resting there as a rope. Soaking wet, he tumbled into her window.

Chintamani pitied him.

She said,

"You're so much attached to this lowly bag of flesh and bones. Better you become attached to serving the blissful Lord Govinda. Go to Vrndavana and there you will find complete satisfaction and eternal happiness."[1]

Vrndavana is the site of Krishna's pastimes when he had descended unto Earth as an avatara of Vishnu. It became a holy *kshetra*, a pilgrimage site populated by sadhus and others devoted to Krishna.

He realized the truth of her words and immediately departed for Vrndavana to do as she suggested. On the way, he was overcome with lust for the wife of a brahmana. Disgusted by his own lack of self-control, he took the lady's hairpin and gouged out his eyes. He thought it better to never see again rather than be distracted from serving Krishna.

He reached Vrndavana and received *diksha*, initiation. He was particularly expert in describing the pastimes of Radha and Krishna and became known as Lilasuka and also Bilvamangala Thakur. He felt so much bliss just from singing about their *leela*, their cosmic play.

Krishna took special care of this old man who had blinded himself for him. He would bring milk for him and make sure he had a safe resting place. Bilvamangala Thakur did not recognize him at first.

One day, the young boy, Krishna, played the flute for him. Suddenly, he realized that the boy had been Krishna all along. He reached out to touch his hand. Krishna playfully swatted his hand away, laughed, and ran off.

Bilvamangala Thakur sang,

"You can run away from my hand, but you can never leave my heart."

Over time, Bilvamangala Thakur wrote several important devotional books, including *Krishna Karnamrta*. He never forgot Chintamani, who had inspired him to turn around his life. He accepted her as his spiritual master and in many places glorified her name and acknowledged her for having shown him the right path.

17

Leela & Padma

The Yoga Vasistha is a classical text of Hinduism. It contains the story of Leela and Padma, which starts out as a love story that transforms into an enlightenment story. The queen suffers from heartbreak and wants to go back in time and remove the source of her anguish by bringing her husband back to life. Saraswati Devi teaches her a lesson about the nature of reality and life, which channels the queen's anguish into gradual enlightenment.

Once upon a time, King Padma and his wife, Queen Leela, ruled over a large kingdom that extended for thousands of miles. Leela was so attached to her husband that she could not bear the thought of him ever dying. She was so desperate that she consulted with ministers and purohitas to find a way to prevent the death of her husband.

They all told her the same thing. Nobody could confer immortality.

Leela was senseless with grief even while her husband still lived. This is the nature of *moha*, delusive attachment, which engulfs us in grief even before our object of attachment is taken away. This is what Hemalekha was explaining to her husband in Tripura Rahasya — that pleasure cannot be said to pleasure when one day it will be extinguished and replaced with yet another desire.

Leela was not one to be easily dissuaded, though. She began to worship Saraswati Devi, the Goddess of Wisdom. She started to eat only once in three days. She had unshakeable faith that her practice would be successful. After a hundred such three-day fasting cycles had passed, Saraswati appeared before her.

Leela prayed to her for two boons: first, that when her husband died, his *jeeva*, his individual essence, would remain in the palace, and second, whenever Leela prayed to Saraswati, she would appear before her.

Saraswati granted the requested boons and left.

～

MANY YEARS PASSED. King Padma was one day badly wounded on the battlefield and died in the palace soon after. Leela was inconsolable.

The voice of Saraswati spoke, telling Leela to cover the king's dead body with flowers. The body would then not decay and he would remain within the palace. This was Devi's way of fulfilling the first boon.

Leela followed Saraswati's instructions somewhat reluctantly. She was not satisfied with this result and felt this was a bit of trickery on the part of Saraswati.

She called upon Saraswati, who true to the second boon she had granted to Leela, immediately appeared.

"Why do you grieve?" Saraswati asked Leela. "Sorrow is but an illusion."

Leela begged her to tell her where her husband was.

Saraswati explained to her that there were three types of space: the psychological space, the physical space, and the infinite space of consciousness. In the infinite space of consciousness, experienced through *nirvikalpa samadhi*, it would be possible to see and experience the presence of one who may not be in the same physical space.

While Leela was not qualified to go into nirvikalpa samadhi on her own yet, Saraswati blessed her so that within moments of going into meditation Leela was immersed in nirvikalpa samadhi.

In that dimension of infinite consciousness, Leela saw the king and many members of the court. When she emerged out of meditation, she was confused. Was everyone she had seen in that reverie now dead? She summoned all the ministers and officials and discovered that, other than her husband, the others were indeed still alive.

How could they appear in two places at once, Leela wondered. She asked Saraswati which dimension was real—the physical plane on which they were speaking just now or the realm they had visited in meditation.

Saraswati turned the question back to her—which did she consider to be real?

Leela thought the physical plane was real and not the dimension of reality they had witnessed through meditation.

Saraswati gave this as an answer:

"How can the unreal be the effect of the real? The effect is the cause, there is no essential difference. Even in the case of a pot which is able to hold water whereas its cause (Clay) cannot, this difference is due to the co-operative causes. What was the material cause of your husband's birth? For only material effects are produced by material causes.

"Hence, when you find no immediate cause for an effect, then surely the cause existed in the past—memory. Memory is like space, empty. All creation here is the effect of that emptiness—and hence the creation is empty, too. Even as the birth of your husband is an illusory product of memory, I see all this as the illusory and unreal effect of imagination."[1]

Saraswati then proceeded to narrate a story to demonstrate the fundamental unreality of what we consider to be the world but which is in reality devoid of independent existence. She said that in a corner of the mind of the Creator there was a dilapidated shrine covered with a blue dome. The fourteen worlds existed as individual rooms within. There were small anthills which stood for cities, little piles of earth that were mountains, and little pools of water that were oceans.

In a very small corner lived a holy man with his wife and children. One day, he was sitting on top of a hill and saw beneath him a colorful procession passing by headed by the king riding a stately elephant. That holy man who until then had led a frugal existence could not stop the wish arising in his heart, that one day he too would ride a royal elephant like that and be followed by his own army.

Many years passed and the king eventually grew old and died. Because of his wish, he became a mighty king and ruled over a great empire.

Saraswati revealed that this all happened eight days ago

and that man was now her husband, King Padma.

Leela was bewildered. How could eight days equate with all the many years she had spent with her husband?

"All this seems so strange and incredible to me. It is like saying that a huge elephant is bound in the centre of a mustard seed or that in an atom a mosquito fought with a lion, or that there is a mountain in a lotus pod."[2]

THE NEXT MORNING, Saraswati and Leela sat for meditation again. They held hands and traveled to distant places. They rested on top of Mount Meru. They saw the seven sacred mountains; they saw Apsaras sing and dance; they traveled through the various abodes of the various Devas.

Eventually, Saraswati and Leela arrived at that holy man's house. Their son and others were in mourning. Leela wished that they appear as ordinary women in the house, and as soon as she willed it so it happened. Leela touched the son's head spontaneously and removed his sorrow as well as the sorrow of everyone else there.

When they left, Leela asked how it was that they were seen by that family but not by her husband the other day when she saw him ruling over a kingdom. Saraswati explained that before she was clinging to the notion that she was Leela but now she had overcome that strong sense of body-identification.

These experiences and the guidance of Saraswati had

been leading Leela gradually toward enlightenment. She realizes herself that she has indeed gone through so many incarnations—

"Since emerging as a reflection in the infinite consciousness I have had 800 births. Today I see this. I have been a nymph, a vicious human woman, a serpent, a forest tribal woman, and on account of evil deeds I became a creeper, and by the proximity of sages I became a sage's daughter; I became a king, and on account of evil deeds done then, I became a mosquito, a bee, a deer, a bird, a fish; and again I became a celestial, after which I became a tortoise, and a swan, and I became a mosquito again. I have also been a celestial nymph when other celestials (males) used to fall at my feet. Just as the scales of balance seesaw constantly I have also been caught up in the seesaw of this repetitive existence, samsara."[3]

Leela intensely desired to see her husband's other life, where he ruled as a king again. Saraswati and Leela entered that realm and went into his apartments. Saraswati put her hand on his head, causing him to instantly remember everything that had transpired. He asked how it could be possible that he had died just a few days ago but had already lived in this body for over seventy years.

Saraswati replied,

"To an immature and childish person who is confirmed in his conviction that this world is real, it continues to be real—even as a child who believes in a ghost is haunted by it throughout his life. If a person is enamoured of the appearance of the bracelet, he does not see that it is just gold: he who sees the glory of palaces, elephants and cities does not see the infinite consciousness which alone is true."[4]

Saraswati told the king, named King Viduratha in this realm, that he would die in the war but then regain his kingdom from his previous life with Leela. In the meantime, the queen, the wife of King Viduratha, appeared.

Leela was shocked to see that this queen was an exact replica of her. The second Leela (that is how she is referred to in the text) asked Saraswati to grant her the boon that when her husband died, she would accompany him wherever he went.

Saraswati agreed, citing that the queen had worshiped her for such a long time with such intense devotion that she merited the boon. The first Leela asked why she had not been given the same boon.

Saraswati explained with a shrug that boons that are bestowed may come through a Deva or Devi but really it is one's own actions (in thought, speech and physical conduct) that determine the fruits of karma enjoyed or suffered by a person.

The second Leela also asked why King Viduratha could not win this battle. Saraswati explained that he had prayed not for victory in battle but rather for liberation whereas the other king had sought victory in battle. Thus Saraswati was arranging things such that each would obtain what he or she wanted.

This is why we must be careful and thoughtful about what we pray for, what we wish for in our heart of hearts. Our desires create our destiny, eventually.

Saraswati and Leela returned to the room where King Padma's body was being kept. They saw that the second Leela was fanning his body. Saraswati and Leela could see her, but she could not see them.

After some time, Saraswati induced Viduratha's jeeva to enter the king's body. He jerked awake as if he had been sleeping. Leela explained to him all that had happened and the identity of the second Leela.

Saraswati granted her final blessings, assuring the king that he would have a long and prosperous reign, before disappearing. For a long time to come, the subjects of the kingdom marveled at how Leela had gone to the other realm and brought back the second Leela, the king governing with both queens at his side.

Part Seven

Sacrifice

18

Savitri

The story of Savitri is one of the most iconic in all of Hinduism. It is emblematic of the ideals and values that undergird Hindu culture and Indic civilization. It tells the tale of a fearless lady who changes the destiny of her husband, her birth family, and her in-laws through her wit, strength of conviction, and indomitable spirit. Sri Aurobindo's magnum opus, *Savitri*, is inspired by this story which we find in the Mahabharata.

Once, there was a noble and pious king, named Ashvapati. He was dedicated to the welfare of all sentient beings. He was childless. And when he reached old age, this saddened him. He began to observe rigid vows and live a frugal life so he could one day become a father.

Every day, that king offered ten thousand oblations into the fire in worship of Savitri Devi, a form of Saraswati Devi, the Goddess of Wisdom. For eighteen years, King Ashvapati followed this practice, reciting mantras in honor of Savitri Devi for many hours each day.

After the completion of eighteen years, the pleased Savitri Devi emerged from the sacrificial fire and revealed

herself to King Ashvapati. She told him to ask of her any
boon.

The king folded his hands before her. "O Devi, may
many sons be born unto me, worthy of my dynasty!"

Savitri Devi smiled at him. "King, I already knew this
was your wish. I have already spoken to Brahma about this
matter. You will be blessed with a daughter of tremendous
energy. Do not reply. Well-pleased, I convey this message to
you at the command of Brahma, the Grandsire."

The king prostrated before her. "So be it! May this
happen soon!"

Savitri Devi disappeared, and the king reentered his
kingdom and resumed his noble rule. After some time, he
fathered a daughter on his seniormost queen. The child was
born with lotus-like eyes. Joyously, the king performed all
the rites that were to be observed. And in honor of the Devi
who had blessed him and the kingdom, the child was named
Savitri.

When Savitri attained maturity, the people of the
kingdom thought that she was herself a Devi, such was her
beauty and the power of the energy she radiated. She was so
awe-inspiring that no man dared to ask for her hand in
marriage.

One day, after bathing and washing her hair, she
worshiped the family deities and presided over the brahmanas tending to the sacrificial fire. Taking the flowers that
had been offered to the deities, Savitri, as beautiful as
Lakshmi herself, approached her father. Having touched his
feet in respect, she offered to him the flowers from the puja
(worship ceremony).

The king felt sad at the sight of this beautiful daughter
of his who had not yet been matched.

"Daughter, the time has come for me to arrange your

marriage. Yet, no one dares ask me for your hand. I cannot think who could qualify to be your husband. Therefore, I leave the decision to you. Seek for yourself a husband who is your equal. Whomever you desire, tell me. With due deliberation, I shall bestow you upon him."

He instructed his attendants to accompany her and keep her safe. Savitri took her father's blessings and walked out of the palace without hesitation or fear. She ascended a golden chariot and embarked upon her quest to find a suitable husband.

Her first destination was an ashram belonging to royal rishis. She made her prostrations to them and began to roam the forests. She distributed wealth wherever she went. She traveled from one ashram to another, visiting different heritages and conversing with many different rishis, taking their counsel and blessings.

One day, Savitri, accompanied by her father's elderly councilors, returned to her father's palace. The king was at that moment seated in conversation with Narada Muni in the middle of court. She prostrated before them.

As we know by now, Narada Muni loved nothing better than getting all the latest news and gossip. He turned to the king.

"Where had your daughter gone? And from where has she returned? By the way, when will you marry her off now that she has come of age?"

The king explained the situation and asked his daughter to apprise them of who she had chosen, urging her to share everything in detail. Both men leaned forward eagerly to hear from Savitri.

Savitri replied, "Father, among the Shalvas, there is a virtuous king known by the name of Dyumatsena. As the years passed, he became blind. He has only one son. An old

rival took advantage of the king's illness and stole his kingdom. Then the king, with his wife and small child, escaped
into the woods. He began to practice great austerities. His
son, born in the city but raised in the forest, that young man
fit to be wed to me, him have I accepted in my heart as my
husband!"

Narada Muni, who knew everything about everyone,
for whom no one and nothing was unknown, cried out,
"Alas! O King, Savitri has made a grave mistake. She could
not have known this, but she should not have accepted this
man of excellent qualities as her husband."

The king opened his mouth to prompt Narada Muni to
say more, but the rishi needed no encouragement. He kept
going.

"Yes, yes, I know him, this Satyavan. His father is
indeed an honest and noble man, as is his mother. It is for
this reason that the boy has been named after Truth. He
used to love horses as a child. He used to fashion horses out
of clay and draw pictures of horses—"

The king interrupted now. "Well, is this prince ener-
getic and intelligent, full of forgiveness and courage?"

Narada intoned, "In energy, Satyavan resembles the
sun; in wisdom, he is like Brihaspati, the guru of the Devas
himself. He is as brave as Indra and as forgiving as Bhu
Devi, Mother Earth herself!"

The king nodded in satisfaction. "And is this prince
generous in disposition and devoted to the brahmanas? Is he
handsome and kind?"

Narada puffed up in appreciation of the prince. "He is
equal to Sankriti's son, Rantideva, in his generosity of
giving. In truthfulness and devotion to the brahmanas, he is
like Shivi, the son of Ushinara. He is as kind as Yayati and

as beautiful as Chandra Deva, the God of the Moon. Even the Ashwin twins would not outshine him in looks."

The king was now puzzled at Narada Muni's objection to the marriage. "You tell me he is excellent in all qualities. Then what are his defects, if any?"

Narada's head hung in sorrow. "He has only one defect, but that one defect outweighs all of his many virtues. None can overcome that defect. This defect is that, within a year from this day, Satyavan will die."

The king shook his head sadly and exhaled loudly. He had known it was too good to be true. He turned to his daughter.

"Savitri, go and choose another husband for yourself."

Savitri squared her shoulders and faced her father and the rishi calmly.

She said, "Death comes but only once. A daughter can be given away but only once. And only once can a person say that he or she gives something or someone away. I have already selected my husband once. I will not do so twice. Having chosen in my mind, I must express it in words, and then must I act upon it."

Narada Muni was exceedingly pleased. "Truly, the heart of your daughter does not waver! I can see now it will not be possible to make her deviate from this vow. I tell you, in no other person can be found those virtues which dwell in Satyavan. I therefore bless your daughter's marriage to him."

The king nodded. "Your words should never be disobeyed, O Narada Muni! As you are my preceptor, I shall do as you have said."

His work done, Narada Muni disappeared into the skies. The king then began preparing for the wedding. He traveled to the forest where Dyumatsena and his family were staying and formally requested the marriage of Satyavan to his daughter.

Dyumatsena said, "Deprived of our kingdom, living in the woods, we lead a frugal existence. How can your daughter bear this, accustomed as she is to palace life?"

"My daughter knows as well as I do that happiness and sorrow come and go. We have made up our minds. I have bowed to you out of friendship. Do not destroy my hope. We are fit and equal to be allied with each other."

Dyumatsena was pleased to accede to the request. He confessed to King Ashvapati that in the past, while he had still been king, he had hoped one day for their children to marry. Once he had been banished to the forest, he had not felt he had the right to seek her hand for Satyavan any longer.

The marriage took place with great fanfare. Satyavan, Savitri, and their parents were full of joy.

AFTER HER FATHER LEFT, Savitri discarded all of her ornaments. She dressed herself in bark dyed red. She looked after her new family and her husband. Everyone adored her. She was ever cheerful but could never forget the ominous words spoken by Narada Muni. Night and day, his words haunted her as the time passed and the approaching death of her husband drew near.

She counted the days as they passed. When only four days remained before the hour of Satyavan's death, Savitri undertook the Triratra vow, fasting day and night for three nights.

When he heard of her vow, Satyavan's father became sorrowful. He spoke to her and urged her not to do it, as she was the daughter of a king, and this was an exceedingly difficult fast. She assured him that it would not be a problem for her. He gave her his blessings for the completion of the fast.

After three days, Savitri began to look like a wooden doll. Thinking that her husband would die the next day, Savitri spent the last night of her fast in extreme anguish. As the dawn approached, Savitri finished her morning rites and made offerings to the rising sun. She bowed down to the elderly brahmanas, to her father-in-law and mother-in-law, and to all those who resided in that ashram.

All the sadhus dwelling there knew the truth of the matter. They cared for Savitri and out of compassion for her, they uttered benedictions that she should never suffer the pain of widowhood. Savitri, immersed in contemplation, heard and accepted those words, saying to herself, "So be it!"

Her parents-in-law urged her to eat now that dawn had come and the new day had arisen. The time to break her fast had arrived. Savitri vowed instead that she would eat only at sunset.

Hearing Savitri's words, Satyavan took his axe upon his shoulders and set out for the woods. He had to collect the wood for the sacrificial fires and other rites.

Savitri cried out to him. "Do not go into the woods alone! I will accompany you. I cannot bear to be separated from you."

Satyavan was surprised. "You have never come with me into the depths of the forest before. The path is difficult to navigate. And you are weakened from your fast. How then can you walk with me into the forest?"

Savitri brushed off his objections and insisted she would

go with him. Satyavan consented on the condition that she obtain permission from his parents.

Savitri addressed her parents-in-law. She told them that the only reason she was allowing him to go to the woods on this day was because it was his duty to collect the materials for the sacrificial rites. Otherwise, she said, she would not have allowed him to leave the ashram for any other reason.

She implored them: "I must accompany him today. Do not stop me! I have not asked for anything in this past year. In all this time, I have not ventured outside of this ashram even once." She told them that she wanted to see the blossoming trees in the forest so as not to worry them.

They consented.

Savitri walked into the forest with her husband, smiling on the outside while her heart was constricted with grief inside. They walked through the enchanting forest. The woods were swarmed with peacocks. The trees were decked with flowers. And the crystalline waters of the rivers were roaring and crashing on the banks.

Satyavan pointed out various sights to her.

But Savitri could not look at anything besides her husband.

Satyavan collected fruits and began chopping wood for the sacrificial fire. He began to sweat and got a headache. He called out to Savitri, telling her he was in pain and had grown suddenly tired, no longer able to stand.

Savitri rushed to his side and sat on the ground, putting his head on her lap. She let him sleep, even as she calculated desperately the moments and minutes she had left with him.

In the next moment, she saw a being clad in red attire wearing a diadem approach them. His body was large and as effulgent as the sun. He was dark in complexion with red eyes and carried a noose in his hand. Truly he was dreadful to behold.

He stood beside Satyavan and gazed at him.

~

SAVITRI GENTLY PLACED her husband's head on the leaf-strewn ground, careful to not disturb him. She rose to her feet.

"I take it you are a Deva. Please tell me, revered one, who you are and what is it that you intend to do."

She already knew that it was Yama Deva, the God of Death.

Yama replied to her in a not unkindly voice. "Savitri, you have always been devoted to your husband. You are also a great ascetic. That is why I deign to talk to you. Know me as Yama. The appointed hour for your husband's death has arrived. I shall carry him away, placing his neck in this noose. This is my mission, and I shall not be swayed from it!"

Savitri kept her composure. "I had heard that your servants come to take away mortal beings. Why then, O revered one, have you come in person this time?"

Yama Deva was not usually talkative, but he respected Savitri enough to continue the conversation. "Your husband is full of virtues and beauty. He is a veritable sea of accomplishments. He does not deserve to be taken away by my attendants."

Yama pulled out of the body of Satyavan his inner *purusha*, a person of the size of a thumb, bound him with his vital essence in the noose, and started to move toward the southern direction. Satyavan's body, now a corpse, transformed into a ghastly sight.

Savitri began to follow Yama as he carried away her husband.

He turned to her and told her to go back. "You have fulfilled all your obligations to your husband. You have already come as far as it is possible to come."

Savitri replied, "Wherever my husband goes or is carried, there I shall follow him, always. By the power of my asceticism, my regard for my superiors, my love for my husband, the strength of my observance of vows, as well as by your grace, neither you nor anything else will be able to stop me. By taking those seven steps with him around the sacred fire, we have become eternal friends and companions."

Yama held up his hand. "Enough! Your reasoned words, eloquently articulated, have pleased me. Ask me for a boon. Except for the life of your husband, I can provide any boon that you wish."

Savitri was quick-witted and did not hesitate. "Deprived of his kingdom and his eyesight, my father-in-law leads a restricted life in the forest. Let him regain his eyesight and become as strong as the fire or the sun."

Yama was anxious to grant her this boon and be on his way. "So be it! You seem tired. Do now turn back and return, O lady of faultless features."

Savitri replied promptly, unwilling to let Yama move any further.

"What weariness can I feel in the company of my husband? That which is his fate is also mine. Wherever you take him, there will I go! Do listen to me, O great Deva! Even a single conversation with the pious is highly desirable. Friendship with them is even more so desirable. A conversation with the virtuous can never be fruitless. One should always live in the company of the righteous."

Yama Deva's heart melted a little bit, despite himself. He rarely found company as wise, noble, and pious as Savitri. Usually, people who had lost their loved ones were too consumed with their grief to be able to carry on such an intelligent conversation.

Reluctantly, the words tumbled out of his mouth.

"Your words delight the heart and increase the wisdom even of enlightened ones. Solicit a second boon of me, anything except for the life of Satyavan!"

Savitri had her answer ready. "Some time ago, my father-in-law was deprived of his kingdom. May that king regain his throne. And may he never abdicate his duties. This is the second boon I seek."

Yama confirmed, "He will soon obtain his kingdom once more. Nor will he ever fall from his duties. Now! Return. Do not create any further trouble."

Savitri persisted. "It is by your decree that creatures live and die. It is not your desire but the laws which you have established. It is by your laws that mortals are taken away from this world. It is for this reason that you are known as Yama Deva!

"The eternal duty for the good of all creatures is to never injure them in thought, word, or deed, but rather to love them and give them their due. In this world, man has become as empty and hollowed out as the corpse of my husband. Men lack both devotion and competence. The noble ones, however, show mercy even to their enemies when they seek refuge."

Yama smiled. "As water to the thirsty, so are your profound words to me! If you will, O fair lady, ask me once more for any boon, anything except Satyavan's life!"

Savitri smiled too. "My father is without sons. May a

hundred sons be born to his line so that his dynasty may be perpetuated. This is the third boon I seek of you!"

Yama agreed. "Indeed, your father, O auspicious lady, shall obtain a hundred illustrious sons who will perpetuate and enhance his line. Now, stop! You have come far enough."

Savitri took another few straggling steps.

"Staying by the side of my husband, I am not even aware how far I have walked. Let us keep going. Listen to my words, O Deva! You are known as Vaivaswata by the wise. Since you dole out the law equally among all created beings, you are also the God of Justice. One cannot have, even in oneself, the confidence that one has in the righteous. That is why everyone wishes to be in the company of the righteous. It is only the goodness of one's heart that inspires the confidence of all creatures. It is for this that people rely especially on the righteous."

Yama shook his head in admiration. It was rare for him to hear appreciation or praise from others, and it touched him more than he cared to admit.

"O fair lady, the words that you have uttered I have not ever, in so many millions of years, heard from anyone else. I am highly pleased with this speech of yours. Except for the life of Satyavan, ask of me a fourth boon, and then be on your way!"

Savitri replied, "Both of me and Satyavan's loins, begotten by both of us, let there be born one hundred strong and powerful sons, capable of perpetuating our line! This is the fourth boon I would seek of you."

Yama promised, "You will certainly obtain one hundred sons, strong and powerful, sons who will bring you great delight. O, daughter of a king, now stop. You have come too far!"

Savitri spoke once more. "They who are righteous always practice righteousness. The interaction of the pious with the pious can never be fruitless. Nor can the pious ever pose danger to those who are pious. Truly it is the righteous who by their truthfulness permit the sun to move in the heavens. It is the righteous who support the earth by their austerities. O king, it is upon the righteous that both the past and future depend! They who are righteous are ever cheerful in the company of the righteous. Knowing this, they who are righteous continue to do good to others without expecting anything in return. The righteous become the protectors of all."

Yama cocked his head to look at her. "The more you talk, the more you deliver these pithy speeches full of honeyed phrases, imbued with righteousness, the more I respect you. O, you who are so devoted to your husband, ask me for some incomparable boon!"

This time, he did not add any conditions.

Savitri bowed her head. "O, bestower of honors, the boon you have already granted me is not capable of being fulfilled without my union without my husband. But for the sake of completeness, among the other boons, I ask that Satyavan be restored to life. Without my husband, I do not wish for happiness. Without him, I do not wish for Swarga or prosperity. You have given me the boon of one hundred sons, yet you take away my husband! I ask that Satyavan be restored to life so that your words will be made true."

Yama pronounced, "So be it."

He untied the noose and with a cheerful heart said to Savitri, "Thus, O auspicious lady, is your husband freed by me. You will be able to take him back free from disease. The two of you shall live together for four hundred years. He will achieve great fame in this world. You will bear him one hundred sons, and all of them will be kings who will always be famous in connection with you. Your father will also father one hundred sons under the name of the Malavas."

Having bestowed these boons on Savitri, Yama departed from the mortal world.

~

SAVITRI RUSHED BACK to the place where Satyavan's ash-colored corpse lay. She sat down on the ground and put his head back on her lap. Satyavan regained consciousness and felt as if he had woken after a long nap.

"Why did you not awaken me, my dear? I have been sleeping a long time! Where is that person, that being of terrible appearance, who was dragging me away?"

Savitri looked away for a moment, thinking of Yama Deva, and turned back to her husband.

"You have been sleeping on my lap for a long time! That restrainer of creatures, that Yama Deva worthy of worship, has gone away. Now rise! The night has come."

Satyavan grew worried. "I came with you to collect fruit. While I was chopping wood, my head started hurting. I was no longer able to stand. And so I lay down on the ground. All of this I remember. I remember being asleep, then it was dark everywhere. In the midst of that darkness, I saw a person of great effulgence. Is what I saw a dream or reality?"

Savitri promised to tell him everything in the morning. She urged him to rise to his feet so that they could go back to his parents. The beasts of the forest were on the prowl. Jackals were howling, making her heart tremble in fear, she said. She did not want to stay in the forest any longer.

Satyavan reported that he was feeling better now. He

recollected how his parents used to worry if he had not returned to them by twilight. He did not want to worry them any further. He became worried about them; they could even die out of concern for him if they did not hear from him soon.

Savitri comforted him. "If I have observed austerities, if I have given gifts and wealth away in charity, if I have performed sacrifices, may this night pass auspiciously for the good of my father-in-law, my mother-in-law, and my husband! I do not remember ever having uttered a lie, even as a joke. Let my father-in-law and mother-in-law maintain their lives on the strength of Truth!"

Savitri helped Satyavan rise and carried the axe for him. Placing his left arm upon her left shoulder, holding him with her right arm, slowly they proceeded on the forest paths shrouded in darkness. They proceeded toward the hermitage.

IN THE MEANTIME, Dyumatsena regained his sight. He proceeded with his wife to all the nearby ashrams in search of his son and daughter-in-law. They searched the ashrams, the rivers, the forests, and the flooded plains. But they could not find him anywhere. Their feet became cracked and wounded, pierced with thorns and the sharp blades of Kusha grass.

The brahmanas from nearby flocked to their side, comforted them, and brought them back to their own ashram. They distracted the couple with stories of ancient kings and queens from the past.

Still, the old couple could not forget their anxiety and soon began wailing in lamentation for Satyavan and Savitri.

One of the brahmanas, named Suvarchas, said, "Considering the austerities, self-restraint, and noble conduct of Savitri, there can be no doubt that Satyavan lives."

Gautama then said, "I have studied all the Vedas in all their branches. I have lived in complete brahmacharya, celibacy. I have pleased Agni Deva and my elders. I have observed all the vows and strictures. I have often lived on air alone. I am always aware of the doings of all others. Take my word for it that Satyavan lives."

His student chimed in. "The words that have been spoken by my guru can never be false. Therefore, Satyavan surely lives on."

Like this, all the rishis echoed each other, confirming that Satyavan and Savitri must be alive.

The aged parents of Satyavan were comforted by the assurances of the rishis.

In some time, that very night, Savitri and Satyavan reached home. The brahmanas saw them. Wishing them all well, they lit a fire and sat in front of King Dyumatsena.

Saivya, his wife, Satyavan, and Savitri stood to the side.

The brahmanas inquired of Satyavan why it had taken them so long to return. Satyavan relayed all that he could remember.

Gautama smiled mysteriously. "So, you know not how and why your father regained his eyesight. It behooves Savitri to tell us. I wish to hear it from you, O Savitri, since I know you to be like Savitri Devi herself in splendor. If it should not be a secret, do not keep it from us!"

Savitri understood that the great rishi knew what had happened. She told all the rishis assembled there, she told her parents-in-law and her husband, all the details of what had transpired, starting from Narada Muni's warning of her husband's impending death.

The rishis applauded and honored with reverence Savitri, that best of women. Then they departed from the ashram with cheerful hearts back to their abodes.

IN THE MORNING, tidings came that the enemy of Dyumatsena had been slain by his own minister. All of that enemy's troops had fled, and his former subjects had unanimously clamored for the throne to be restored to Dyumatsena. They did not care whether he was blind or not. He would always be their king.

A special chariot, escorted by his army, had been sent to bring back the king. The king honored the elderly and the brahmanas who resided in the ashram where he and his family had made their home for so long. Then he set out for his city, accompanied by his family. Dyumatsena was successfully installed on the throne, with Satyavan crowned as the prince-regent.

In time, Savitri did indeed give birth to one hundred sons, all fierce and brave warriors. She also gained one hundred brothers from King Ashvapati. This is how that greatest of women, Savitri, not only raised herself from a place of great calamity to a place of great fortune but also transformed the fates and lives of her parents, her parents-in-law, her husband, and the dynasties into which she was born and wed.

Ruru & Pramadvara

In India and among Hindus, the story of Savitri is much more well-known than the story of Ruru and Pramadvara, even though Ruru also fights against the demise of his beloved and pleads with an emissary of Yama Deva to extend her life. So, it is inspirational to read this story in connection with the story of Savitri.

We have already covered the story of Chyavana of the Bhrigus and his wife, Sukanya. They bore a son named Pramati. And Pramati, through Ghrtachi, fathered a son called Ruru. Ruru also eventually fathered a son, Sunaka, with his wife, Pramadvara. This is the story of Ruru and Pramadvara.

Once, there was a great rishi named Sthulakesha. He was kindly disposed to all creatures and possessed much ascetic power. It is said that Viswavasu, the king of the Gandharvas, had been intimate with Menaka, an Apsara whose affair with Vishwamitra we read about earlier.

Menaka gave birth near the ashram of Sthulakesha. Not for the only time, she left the baby on the banks of the river. Menaka then left without another thought. Sthulakesha saw that baby abandoned by the river. He saw that it was a girl, blazing with beauty. Filled with compassion, he raised the child and performed all the birth and childhood ceremonies and rites that were prescribed. The rishi named her Pramadvara because she exceeded all other females in learning, beauty, and good character.

Ruru once saw Pramadvara in Sthulakesha's ashram, and his heart was pierced with love. Taking the advice of his friends, Ruru conveyed to his father, Pramati, his feelings for Pramadvara.

Pramati, eager to make his son happy, requested her hand from that great rishi, Sthulakesha. Their wedding was thus set for the day when Purva-Phalguni or Varga-Daivata would be ascendant.

A few days before their wedding, Pramadvara was playing with her girlfriends when she stepped upon a coiled serpent. Impelled by fate, that snake pierced its fangs into her body and the poison spread through her quickly. She collapsed on the ground, lifeless.

Sthulakesha and all the other rishis who were in the area gathered around her. Renowned sages like Swastyatreya, Mahajana, Kushika, Sankhamekhala, Uddalaka, Katha, Bharadwaja, Kaunakutsya, Arshtishena, Gautama, and Shweta all came in their compassion for the grief of Sthulakesha and Ruru. Pramati, Ruru's father, also came. All the inhabitants of the forest, human and animal, came to see her. They all wept at the sight of her.

But Ruru, who could not bear the pain of her death, fled the scene. He went deep into the woods, where nobody could find him, and gave into his grief. He wept aloud. He wailed and he lamented.

When finally he could speak, Ruru cried out, "Alas! That lovely girl lies upon the cold ground. What can be more devastating to us, her friends? If I have been charitable, if I have performed austerities, if I have honored my elders and superiors, then let the merit accrued thereby restore the life of my beloved Pramadvara! If from birth I have controlled my passions and maintained my vows, then let Pramadvara rise from the ground, life and health restored."

Eventually, a messenger came from the abode of Yama Deva.

He said to Ruru, "Your words are ineffective, O Ruru. One whose time has come, such a one cannot be brought back to life. This pitiable daughter of a Gandharva and Apsara has run out of days. Do not sorrow, young man. The Devas have already arranged a method by which her life may be restored. If you follow it, then you may obtain once again your Pramadvara."

Ruru eagerly took up his offer. "O, messenger! Tell me in full so that I may immediately do what is necessary. Deliver me from grief!"

The messenger replied, "Give up half of your life for your bride, Pramadvara, and if you do so, then your Pramadvara shall indeed rise from the ground."

Ruru readily accepted. "O, best of celestial messengers, I happily give up half my life for the sake of my bride. Let her rise up once more."

Then, the messenger, joined by Pramadvara's father, the king of the Gandharvas, left Earth to approach Yama Deva.

They said to him, "If it be your will, Dharmaraja, let Pramadvara, the betrothed wife of Ruru, rise from death in exchange for half of Ruru's prescribed lifetime."

Yama consented. "If that be your wish, then let it be so."

At his utterance of those words, Pramadvara rose as if

from sleep. In time, she and Ruru were married to each other under the watchful gaze of Pramati and Sthulakesha. They passed their days in affectionate harmony, devoted to each other. Ruru knew he had obtained a wife of rare beauty and qualities, the like of whom could not easily be found in the world.

RURU NEVER REGRETTED HIS SACRIFICE, but he never forgot or forgave the snake who had attacked his wife. Any time he saw a snake, he would become enraged and kill it. He even took a vow to destroy the entire species of serpents, so thirsty was he for vengeance.

One day, Ruru entered a large forest. He saw an old snake of the dundubha variety lying on the ground before him. In anger, Ruru lifted his staff to strike at him.

The dundubha snake spoke to Ruru. "I have done you no harm, O brahmana! Why will you then kill me for no reason?"

Ruru kept his staff raised. "My wife, as beloved to me as my own life, was bitten by a snake. And so I took a vow that I would kill every snake I encounter."

The aged snake hissed in a way that made it seem like he was laughing.

"O brahmana, there are so many different types of snakes. You should not slay dundubhas, who are not venomous. Alas, dundubhas, the variety of snakes to which I belong, suffer the misfortunes common to all serpents but have not their powers. The dundubhas should not be killed by you out of your misconceptions."

Ruru saw that the old snake was frightened of him, and,

stirred by his words, lowered his staff and refrained from killing him. He befriended that old dundubha snake.

"Tell me, who are you? And how did it come to be that you were transformed into a snake that could talk?"

The dundubha snake shared his story.

"Once, I was a rishi named Sahasrapat. By the curse of a brahmana I was changed into a snake. I used to have a friend named Khagama. He was impulsive in speech. One day, he was performing the *Agnihotra* rite (daily rite made through the sacrificial fire). As a joke, I made a fake snake by twisting together blades of grass. I tried to frighten him with it during his worship. He fainted in fear. When he regained consciousness, he was furious and cursed me that just as I had used a fake snake to frighten him, I would be turned into a venom-less serpent.

"He had always been a hothead and was shaking in rage. I apologized to him. I explained that it was just meant to be a joke and asked him to withdraw the curse. He thought about it and started to feel badly for me, I could tell. He told me that when Ruru, the pure son of Pramati, would appear, then would I be freed of his curse. Now that you are here, once I regain my human form I will tell you something for your own good."

The rishi transformed back into his original radiant human form. He then said to the amazed Ruru:

"O thou first of created beings, verily the highest virtue of man is sparing the life of others. Therefore, a brahmana should never take the life of any creature. A brahmana should ever be mild. This is the most sacred injunction of the Vedas. A brahmana should be versed in the Vedas and Vedangas, and should inspire all creatures with belief in God. He should be benevolent to all creatures, truthful, and forgiving, even as it is his paramount duty to retain the Vedas in his memory. The duties of the kshatriya are not thine. To be stern, to wield the sceptre and to rule the subjects properly are the duties of the kshatriya."[1]

Their conversation goes on.

20

The Dust of the Gopis' Feet

Narada Muni had an insatiable curiosity. He was fond of asking all kinds of questions and testing mortals and immortals alike. Once, he asked Krishna to show him who was his greatest devotee.

This, thought Narada, would be tough even for Krishna to answer. Who was there in the world who did not love Krishna? Even the cows and deer of his native Vrndavana followed him wherever he went as a child; even the leaves of the branches of the trees bent toward him, longing for his glance and to touch his body. And, of course, there were his sixteen thousand plus wives. He was the all-attractive one, after all. Narada Muni himself was an ardent devotee of Krishna.

So, thought the rishi, this would be a difficult challenge indeed. How to choose the best of those who loved Krishna?

When Narada posed the question, Krishna reclined on the soft cushions of his couch and closed his eyes with a smile.

Narada thought it seemed as if he already knew the answer.

Krishna's brow suddenly furrowed and he rubbed his forehead and massaged his scalp, setting his crown askew. He began moaning in pain. Narada was alarmed to see his beloved Krishna fall sick. He ran to his side and asked what he should do to help.

Krishna complained that his headache was unbearable. Narada leapt to the door, summoning the guards, calling out for the *vaidyas*, practitioners of medicine, *purohitas*, and healers to immediately come treat Krishna.

Krishna waved them all away. He lay his arm across his eyes as if it was too unpleasant for him to look at the world. He crooked his finger, adorned with a gem-encrusted ring, at Narada and summoned him to his side.

"Listen. There is only one cure for that which ails me. Bring me the dust of the feet of my devotee, of one who loves me."

Narada's jaw dropped. Not only was this a most peculiar request but it was scandalous. To take the dust of one's feet was equivalent to that person putting their foot on Krishna's head. There was no one in the three worlds qualified to have their feet touched by the head of Krishna. Such a disrespectful gesture would consign anyone who dared it to a hellish existence for a very long time indeed.

Narada protested and asked for some other alternative. But Krishna had become non-responsive, as if he had fallen unconscious, grunting every now and then as the pain kept growing in intensity.

Narada Muni ran out of the palace, vowing to find the cure for Krishna. He traveled to many different places, searching for one who would give the dust of his or her feet to remove Krishna's headache.

He begged all the rishis and yogis he met; he solicited the help of Krishna's closest ministers and attendants.

Everyone was eager to help, but as soon as they heard what the cure was, they shrank back. It was too great a sin, they said. They could not disrespect their revered Krishna like that.

Even Krishna's wives refused. They explained to Narada that to do so would be a betrayal of their duties as the wives of Krishna; they were bound to always honor and respect him. They would not give up their virtue as the wives of Krishna.

Narada began to despair.

Finally, he went to Vrndavana to approach the *gopis*, the cowherd girls with whom Krishna had grown up, whom he had left behind when he left for Mathura and later Dwaraka to become a prince and a king and fulfill the destiny for which he had incarnated as an avatara of Vishnu on Earth.

As soon as the gopis saw Narada, they rushed to greet him, thinking he may have news for them about Krishna. Since he had left Vrndavana, the gopis and Krishna had no contact and had not met again for so many years.

Narada quickly explained to them about Krishna's headache. They were devastated to hear of his suffering. Before he could broach the subject of the cure he sought, the gopis impatiently demanded of him answers on how to heal Krishna.

Narada was wary of having to go through this exercise again. He hesitantly told them that Krishna's headache would be cured if the dust of their feet was applied to his head. Instantly, the gopis ran away from Narada toward the banks of the Yamuna River.

Narada hung his head in dejection. Had he offended them so deeply that they could not even bother to tell him no? Had he chased them away with his impertinence? He had not met with the gopis before, but he knew that the intensity of their feelings for Krishna was unmatched.

Narada looked up to see that the gopis were wetting their feet in the water of the Yamuna. Then they started rolling their feet on the ground to collect as much dust as possible. Again and again they repeated this procedure until heaps of dust had been piled together for Narada.

Narada was rarely speechless, but he was at a loss of words witnessing the actions of the gopis.

He asked them, "Don't you know that if Krishna applies the dust of your feet on his head, then all of you would suffer in hell?"

The gopis laughed at him, as if he were a silly man asking a stupid question.

"If by any act of ours we can please Krishna, if we can do good for him, even for a moment, then we would happily suffer in hell for eternity. We want only Krishna's happiness, nothing else."

At that moment, Narada Muni realized that truly the love of the gopis for Krishna was unparalleled. He collected the dust and rushed back to Dwaraka. He flung open the heavy golden doors to Krishna's bedchamber. Krishna was still where he had left him, lying on the couch in a deep sleep.

Narada knelt by his side and prepared to put bits of the dust from the gopis' feet on his forehead.

Immediately, Krishna's eyes opened and shone with merriment as he looked at Narada. He smiled as if he had never been sick in the first place.

"Do you have your answer now?" Krishna asked.

Narada chuckled, realizing this had all been Krishna's leela, his play, to glorify the love and devotion of the gopis.

"Indeed, I do," Narada said with a smile.

Part Eight

Separation

Note

A major and recurring theme across Hindu love stories is separation. Separation is not just a cause of suffering; it becomes an integral aspect and component of love. In some bhakti traditions, love as experienced through separation becomes glorified as one of the highest of bhavas, or modes of experience conducive to devotion and ultimate union with one's ishta devata, one's chosen form of the Divine.

The prime archetypal couple in Hinduism is Shiva and Shakti. The very first story of this collection, the story of Ardhanarishvara, is dedicated to them. Even that most exalted of couples faced separation for a long time, for many, many, many years, after Sati cast off her body when Shiva had been insulted by her father.

Separation is not just for suffering. The trials brought about through the pain of missing one's beloved, whether in the case of the Devas or mortals, test and strengthen the relationship and bring about growth.

21

The Story of the Crow

The Poet has no words good enough to describe the closeness of the union, of the ways in which husband pleased wife and wife pleased husband. . . . They read each other's thoughts readily; in fact these told each other what they wanted. The tongue and the lips did not play any part nor perhaps did the eyes; heart spoke to heart. Hridaya and hridaya commingled. The desire of each was known to the other. It is difficult to say who loved whom the more.

We have seen already that the love that drew Rama and Sita together was most remarkable. When she was lost to him there was no limit to the grief that he bore . . . . He could not find any rest being away from her. He nearly went mad. He wandered from place to place in the forest. He raved. He implored the trees and hills and rivers. He threatened the gods with destruction of the world. He threatened to take his own life. Lakshmana was hard put to it to comfort him in this extreme sorrow.[1]

— *Rt. Hon. V.S. Srinivasa Sastri, from*
Lectures on the Ramayana

In the Ramayana, one of the two Itihaasa epics of Bharat alongside the Mahabharata, Rama and Sita, the romantic couple at the heart of the tale, have been tragically separated. Sita was abducted by the Rakshasa, Ravana, and held captive in Lanka. Rama sent Hanuman on a mission to find her. Hanuman through his intelligence and powers found Sita and was able to meet with her. He introduced himself to her and told Sita that he would immediately take her away from Lanka and to her husband's side.

Then began a long discussion between Hanuman and Sita. Sita explained all of her reasons for not going back with Hanuman, insisting that Rama must be the one to take her back home.

Hanuman requested that, if she was not willing to go with him, she at least give him a token of remembrance to give to Rama.

Sita then narrated the story of the crow, her voice trembling with suppressed tears. This is the speech she gave to Hanuman from the Ramayana:[2]

"There is a place inhabited by the rishis on a hillside. It is a beautiful part of the forest, full of fruit trees and water bodies. We were staying at an ashram there, once long ago during our period of exile. We walked through groves fragrant with flowers and by rivers and lakes shining under the sunlight.

"Tell him, O Hanuman, to remember that time when we were resting together, his head in my lap as he was napping. A crow, a strange crow, started pecking at me. I threw some dirt at him to stop him. Pecking at me again and again, that bird would not desist. Fighting with the bird, my dress slipped, and I was tightening it when Rama awoke and saw me in this state.

"I took refuge in Rama's arms and rested in his lap, even as he laughed at me for being silly. I pretended to be angry but was secretly delighted at how he teased me and how tenderly he held me in his arms.

"For a long time, I slept in his lap, tired as I was from fighting off the crow. Rama, too, slept in my arms. Suddenly, the crow flew down at me and clawed at the space between my breasts. That bird repeatedly scratched my flesh until he drew blood.

"I did not want to disturb the slumber of my husband. But when Rama felt the drops of blood fall on his face, he jerked awake to see the blood marks on my body. The sight of even that slight injury made him hiss like an angry serpent.

"'Who has wounded you, O Sita? Who dares to play with me, a fire-faced serpent filled with fury at the sight of his wife attacked?'

"Rama's eyes fell upon the crow whose claws were dripping with my blood. He was no ordinary crow. He appeared to be no less than the son of Indra, climbing to the heights of the mountains and moving as fast as the wind. My husband's eyes swirled with anger. He would not let the crow go unpunished.

"Taking a blade of Kusha grass from the mat on which we were resting, Rama chanted over it and transformed it into Brahma's missile, which was empowered with infallible destruction. Its aim was unfailing. That blazing grass blade flared up in front of the crow, looking as if it would burn up the world.

"The crow flew this way and that, trying to evade the missile. But wherever it went, the missile was hot on its tail. Like this, that missile dispatched by my husband chased the crow all over the world.

"Searching the three worlds for a protector, the crow was abandoned by Indra, the other Devas, and the rishis. Finally, the harried crow sought refuge in Rama, the one who sought to destroy him in the first place.

"But my husband is always compassionate and always protects those who seek shelter at his feet. Rama smiled upon the crow, whose black skin was trembling with fear and exhaustion. Rama told him that it was not possible to counteract the missile. He asked the crow what he wanted to be done. The crow requested that the missile shoot him in his right eye. Losing one eye, the crow was able to save his own life. The crow then bowed before Rama and returned to his abode."

Sita took a deep breath. "Share with him my words, Hanuman, as if it is I who am directly addressing him. Tell him I say:

'O, lord of the Earth! For my sake, you shot a missile even at a crow who had annoyed me. Why are you forgiving the one who has taken me away from you? O, Rama! You are so strong, exceptionally skilled in archery, and eternally devoted to the truth. Why then are you not showering your arrows upon the Rakshasas? Neither the Nagas, nor the Gandharvas, nor the Asuras, nor the *Maruts*, the deities of the storm, can resist you on the battlefield. There is no doubt that I must have committed a great sin, otherwise why would you neglect me like this?'"

Hanuman understood the deep anguish of Sita, who had been suffering for so long. He comforted her and assured her that Rama was inconsolable without her and was intent on bringing her back safely. He then asked her for any message to relay to Rama and the others.

Sita, now calmed, said, "On my behalf, salute by bowing your head and ask about the welfare of Rama, the lord of all the worlds, the son of Kausalya."

For Sita, Rama, her beloved husband, always came first, before her own anguish and suffering.

And with that Hanuman left, and the preparations began for the great war which would see the victory of Rama and the homecoming of Rama and Sita back to Ayodhya, the kingdom from which they had been exiled for so long.

22

The Grief of Shiva

There is no divine couple more exalted in Hinduism than Shiva and Shakti. Even they faced long periods of separation from each other in their manifestation as Shiva and Sati. Sati had cast off her body when her father had insulted Shiva. For many, many years, Shiva and Sati had been separated until Sati was finally reborn as Parvati and reunited with Shiva.

For a long time, Shiva—that same Shiva who was the most isolationist of the Devas, who was the Adi Yogi, the fiercest of renunciates—was consumed by grief. He carried the corpse of Sati, wandering across the universe, crazed with fury and sorrow at the loss of his wife. He was so maddened that he sent the universe hurtling on the way to an early annihilation. Finally, Vishnu had to use his Sudarshana Chakra to sever Sati's corpse into pieces.

After that, Shiva retreated into meditation once more. He became lost to the external world. That was when the Devas sent Kamadeva to rouse him into passion, as we read about earlier. It turns out that Kamadeva's arrows did in fact have a powerful effect on Shiva. After incinerating the hapless Kamadeva into a heap of ashes, Shiva cried out for Sati and could not find her anywhere.

Unable to bear the long-buried love and longing revived by those arrows shot expertly by Kamadeva, Shiva ran here and there but could not find any relief. Out of desperation, Shiva jumped into the Kalindi River. The waters of the river became black from the power of his grief. Ever since that day, the river has remained black in color.

23

Separation in Union: The Two Bees

There are two stories related to a bumblebee and Krishna that exemplify the peculiar bhava of the gopis and Radha, who experience the deepest of bhava through the mode of separation in love. The first comes from the Srimad Bhagavata.

Once, Krishna had sent Uddhava, one of his closest associates, to Vrndavana. Krishna wanted him to comfort the family and friends he had left behind in his childhood home, to share with them the news of Krishna that they would be longing to hear. Krishna also wanted Uddhava to appreciate the devotion of the gopis.

As soon as Uddhava appeared in their midst, the gopis asked about Krishna and complained about having been neglected by him for so long. One of the gopis—some believe this to be Radharani, but the Srimad Bhagavata does not specifically name her—does not even notice Uddhava. Her attention is captured by a honeybee. She takes it to be a messenger sent by her beloved Krishna. She delivers an entire speech to that bee who torments her.

She says:[1]

"O honeybee, friend of a cheater, do not touch my feet with your wings, which have been smeared with the saffron that was rubbed onto Krishna's garland when it was crushed by the breasts of a rival lover! Let Krishna satisfy the women of Mathura.

"After making us drink the enchanting nectar of his lips just once, Krishna abandoned us, just as you, O honeybee, may quickly abandon some flowers. How is it, then, that Lakshmi Devi willingly serves his Lotus feet? . . .

"O bee, why do you sing here so much about Krishna, the lord of the Yadavas, in front of us homeless people? This is old news for us. Better you sing about Krishna, that friend of Arjuna, in front of his new female companions, the burning desire in whose breasts he has now relieved. Those ladies will surely give you the charity you are begging.

"In any of the three worlds, what women exist who are unavailable to him? He simply arches his eyebrows and smiles with deceptive charm, and they all become his. . . .

"Keep your head off my feet. I know what you're doing. You learned diplomacy from Krishna, and now you come as his messenger with your flattering words. But he abandoned those who for his sake alone gave up their children, husbands, and all other relations. He's ungrateful. Why should I make up with him now?

"Let us give up all friendship with this dark-complexioned boy, even if we cannot give up talking about him. . . . O messenger, please talk about something besides Krishna. O friend of my dear one, has my beloved sent you here again? I should honor you, friend, so please choose whatever boon you wish. . . ."

The tenth *skandha* (section) of the Srimad Bhagavata contains the most authoritative version of the stories of Krishna's leela. Good English translations are also available from the Sri Ramakrishna Mission and from Gita Press Gorakhpur. There, you can read the full speech made by the gopi to the honeybee and many other wondrous things.

THE SECOND STORY relates to Radha and the bumblebee. In some of the esoteric bhakti traditions associated with Radha-Krishna in Gaudiya Vaishnavism, special attention is given to different bhavas, flavors of moods, including *vipralambha* bhava, the experience of love through the intense feeling of separation.

You may have noticed in the earlier passage where the gopi addresses the honeybee, even as she is complaining about Krishna (this is also referred to as maan-leela, or the bhava of anger which is taken up only to please and glorify the beloved), even as she bewails the distance between them, she is so intent upon remembering him and imagining what he is doing elsewhere at that moment that she feels his presence and is able to evoke his presence more strongly than if he were actually there physically. The *rahasya* (secret) of that is the paradox of vipralambha.

In this conception of love, both *sambhoga* (union) and vipralambha (separation) are present. They are considered the two embankments between which the river of love flows. In Vrndavana, Krishna is *vishaya*, the object of love, and Radha is *ashraya*, the abode of love.

Here we see a duality, but in certain rare instances, we find both combined together. This phenomenon is known as *prema-vaicittya*, where both the feeling of sambhoga (union) and the feeling of vipralambha (separation) coexist. Sri Rupa Goswami, one of the foremost acharyas of Gaudiya Vaishnavism, writes about this.

One example of this can be found in a wondrous leela depicted in the *Vidagdha-madhava*, a sixteenth-century play by Sri Rupa Goswami. Here we find the story of Radha and the bumblebee.

One day, Radha and Krishna were playing on the bank of the Yamuna River. Vrnda Devi brought them two lotus flowers. Vrnda Devi indicated to Krishna that he was to take the white lotus as a toy and the two red lotuses as earrings. Krishna accepted the flowers, delighted that the two red lotuses would make Radha's ears appear even more beautiful.

Krishna smiled at his beloved Radha and was about to place the red lotuses on her ears when he noticed a black bumblebee in the whorl of the white lotus. Radha saw it, too. She grew frightened and swatted ineffectually at the bee, trying to shoo it away.

Krishna laughed at her antics, listening to her bracelets tinkling as she tried to chase away the bee.

He teased her, "The bumblebee hovers around you, and you follow it with your restless eyes, themselves like a swarm of bumblebees. Your fear of this bee brings me great delight, Radharani."

Radha persisted in swatting the bee away. The bumblebee finally left the white lotus flower, but then he saw Radha's face and thought that was a lotus too. Now he buzzed here and there around her face.

Again, Radha shooed it with her hand. The bee then thought that her palm was yet another lotus and flew toward her hand.

Radha cried out, "This mad bumblebee is not leaving. Get out! Get out!"

Krishna kept teasing her. "Oh, sweet girl, do not uselessly wave the edge of your sari at him. Let him drink the honey from the lotus flowers I have attached to your ears."

He used the word *madhumangala*, which was also the name of Krishna's friend, Madhumangala. Madhumangala took this to mean that Krishna wanted the bee to sting him, to distract the bee from the target of Radha.

Saying this, Madhumangala drove away the bee with a stick. The bumblebee suddenly went far away.

Surprised to see this, Madhumangala said, "How did that bee disappear? I don't see him anywhere!"

There is yet another play of words here. The term Madhumangala used—*mahusu-ano*—can be interpreted to mean both the bumblebee and also "the killer of the Madhu Asura," (i.e., Krishna).

Radha, who is always thinking only of Krishna, misunderstood Madhumangala to mean that Krishna had disappeared.

As soon as she heard this, Radha cried out in bewilderment. "Alas! Alas! Where has Krishna gone? The cows must have cried out in pain, frightened of some forest fire. Or did Krishna see some fault in me, so that he has abandoned me in the forest? Has he been called away by another girl? Shall I be left here alone?"

The astonishing part of this was that this whole time that Radha was crying out, suffering from pangs of separation from her beloved, she was actually sitting in his lap. He had never left her side. This is what is known as *prema-vaicittya*.

Krishna smiled, touched with wonder at the intensity of her reaction. With a small gesture of his hand, Krishna dismissed everyone else from that area. Madhumangala and Vrnda Devi left.

As she was walking away, Vrnda Devi muttered, "The

intense bond of prema, love, makes her completely blind to reality."

Radha kept lamenting. "He did not decorate my hair with vasanti flowers. I did not string a garland of champaka flowers to decorate his chest."

Krishna smiled, just kept smiling, and looked at Radha with awe.

Krishna reflected to himself that although she was in his arms, he could not remove her suffering. She was constantly scorched by the fear of impending separation and this made her inconsolable. When he was away from her, she experienced him more intensely, thinking of him always out of separation. In that way, she would even talk to the tamala trees, thinking them to be him. But when he was nearby, when he was at her side, she paradoxically felt greater separation and would become distressed and cry.

He realized that the time had come for him to leave Vrndavana to go far away to Mathura and Dwaraka. Only in that way could he fulfill his destiny and she hers.

This bhava of Radharani is considered to be the most exalted of bhava. In this, mutually opposed moods, like sambhoga and vipralambha are present simultaneously. No one else can do this like Radha.

24

Union in Separation: A Story of Radha, Rukmini & Krishna

The last story was about the experience of separation in union. This beautiful story, again about Radha and Krishna, from the Garga Samhita is about the other side of the coin, the experience of union in separation. This episode describes what happened when for one fleeting day Krishna was reunited with Radha and the other gopis after leaving Vrndavana and marrying Rukmini and his other wives.

The auspicious meeting took place in Siddhashrama. When the gopis saw Krishna arrive with his queens, they called out to him joyously. Radha was silent but she wept silently in bliss of seeing him again as she respectfully circumambulated Krishna, her beloved.

Radha, who was Vrajeshwari, the mistress of the forests of Vraj, had always decorated flower-strewn platforms and swings, riverside pavilions, and sylvan thrones for the enjoyment of Krishna. Now she offered him a throne fit for a king, gem-encrusted, glistening with rubies, and topped with a dome and a parasol that flowed with nectar.

Radha said, "Now my life is a success. Now my austerities are a success." With sweet words, she praised Krishna. She recounted how he had brought her so many friends in this world, all the gopis who had become her sakhis and eternal companions. For their sake, he had revealed his power and glory in Vrndavana. She said that in the dance of the raasa-leela, he had embraced the gopis and had been conquered by the gopis.

At that moment, she was informed of the presence of the queens who were Krishna's wives. She looked at them respectfully and offered her respectful prostrations to each of them, one by one. She joyously met with Rukmini, Jambavati, Satyabhama, Satya, Bhadra, Lakshmana, Kalindi, Mitravinda, and all of his other queens. She embraced them all.

She said to them sweetly, "As there is but one moon but the chakora birds are many; as there is but one sun but the eyes are so many; so also, there is but one Krishna but we devotees, my sisters, are many.

"O queens, as a bumblebee understands the glory of lotus flowers, as a jeweler understands the glory of jewels, as a scholar understands the glory of knowledge, as a poet understands the glory of poetry, and as a person expert at tasting nectar understands the glory of the nectar, so only a devotee of Krishna can truly understand the glory of Krishna."

Rukmini replied after listening to Radharani's charming words. "O Radha, you are fortunate. Krishna is conquered by your love. He is under your control. The three worlds glorify Krishna, but Krishna glorifies you."

Rukmini invited Radha to come to her pavilion and respectfully accompanied her along the way. She made Radha comfortable. The pavilion was named Sarvatobhadra, which was fragrant with lotuses and other flowers and covered with soft cushions. Rukmini and all the queens served the gopis and Radha and made sure they were all comfortable, tending to the hundreds and hundreds of gopis one by one. The queens waited until each gopi was comfortably sleeping.

By this time, it was quite late at night. Rukmini saw that Krishna was still awake. She went to him and asked why he had not yet fallen asleep.

Krishna spoke to her tenderly. "My dear wife, you with the beautiful eyebrows, Radha was very pleased by the respectful welcome you gave her. She always drinks milk before she sleeps. Since you have not arranged that milk for her to drink, she is unable to fall asleep. And, O noble-hearted girl, if she cannot sleep, I cannot sleep."

Rukmini immediately brought a golden vessel filled with hot milk and sweetened with sugar to Radha. She offered her some betel nuts too.

Rukmini returned to Krishna's side and reported what she had done. She bent to touch his feet before retiring for the night. As she massaged her husband's feet with her soft hands, Rukmini was shocked to see that the soles of Krishna's feet were covered with blisters.

She cried out to see his feet injured like this.

"How could this have happened? I cannot understand the reason."

As all the queens and wives of Krishna listened, Krishna explained the matter to Rukmini. He wished to show them all the depth of Radha's love.

He said, "Day and night, my feet reside in Radha's lotus heart. Bound by ropes of love and devotion, they cannot stray from her heart even for a moment or even for half a second. She, too, is always worshiping my feet in her heart and immersed only in thought of me. The milk you gave her was far too hot for her delicate constitution. When her throat was scalded by the hot milk, she did not even notice because she is only ever thinking of me. But as for me, who am always thinking of her, my feet became burned. Whatever she feels, I feel. Her pain becomes my own and no longer hers."

Rukmini and the other beautiful queens were wonderstruck. They perceived the greatness of Radha, who was ever devoted to Krishna, and the greatness of Krishna, who was ever in the heart of his devotee. This is the purest form of love; this is the greatest love.

Part Nine

Leela

Note

Sometimes, in a moment of existential doubt, we ask ourselves why are we here, why are we alive, why did the Divine create this world of suffering and impermanence. It is the conditioning of our mind to always seek cause and effect, to ascribe order and linearity to things. But what the sages, the wise ones, the great ones tell us is: there is no why.

There is a famous verse from the Brahma Sutras, one of the trio of texts (*prasthana traya*) that constitute the metaphysical and ontological foundation of Vedanta in the Hindu tradition. The verse proclaims:

> *Lokavat tu lila kaivalyam (The creation is but the play of Brahman).*[1]

The Brahman referred to in this verse is not the same as the brahmana, a member of the priestly class traditionally dedicated to gathering and spreading Vedic knowledge and practice. This Brahman is the non-dual consciousness which pervades all; when it takes on qualities, it manifests as Iswara, as Bhagavan or Bhagavati, as Vishnu or Krishna or Rama or Shiva or Devi. When Brahman remains attribut-eless, it is the impersonal (*nirguna*) Brahman.

The verse points to the fact that Bhagavan or Brahman is always complete and does not need to create creation. There is no dependence and hence no causation. It is all to be understood as leela, as play and sport that is spontaneous.

When it comes to love, too, while so many of the stories we have covered here have thematic significance and teach us important lessons, impart values to us, and crystallize within our minds a worldview and philosophical outlook on the meaning and purpose of life—while all this is true, it would be a mistake to look at these stories in such a reduc-tionist and black-and-white way.

Sometimes, love is just love. Sometimes, love is just leela. And we should celebrate that too.

25

Peacock Leela

Today, if you travel to Vraj in India, a half-a-day drive from New Delhi, if you drive to Barsana Dham, the birthplace of Radharani, if you climb one of the hills there, you will come across an extraordinary small temple known as Mayura Kutira. The word *mayura* refers to peacocks. This is an extraordinarily powerful place and the site of one of the most beautiful leelas enacted by Radha and Krishna.

This is where Radha and Krishna danced many times as peacocks.

Once, it was the monsoon season. Radha saw the peacocks and peahens in that area. They craned their necks to watch the dark gray clouds slung low across the sky as they danced together. Radha was captivated by the sight and conveyed her wish to be like the peacocks and peahens to Krishna. Immediately, Krishna took the form of a peacock and she took the form of a peahen and they danced together on top of the hill.

Another time, Krishna asked Radha to teach him how to sing. She was a wonderful singer. In fact, out of her desire to please Krishna in all ways, Radha had mastered the sixty-four sacred arts. Her voice was as sweet as a cuckoo bird. In fact, it was sweeter than the sound of the cuckoo bird. When they heard her, even the cuckoo birds tried to sing like Radharani. And so Krishna asked her to teach him also.

Every time she sang, Krishna was enchanted. He did not want the lesson to end so he would always sing the song she was teaching him slightly off-key. That way, she was forced to keep extending the lesson until he learned properly. She kept teaching him, and the classes would never end.

One day, Radha caught on to Krishna's tricks. She became angry and went to Maan Mandir, the temple of anger, which was located on the hill opposite to the hill where the Mayura Kutira would one day be built. She refused to talk to Krishna. She would not even look at him. Krishna was anxious to win back her company.

He went to the top of the hill that faced Maan Mandir and began dancing in the form of a peacock. Radharani could not resist looking at him. The dance of Krishna was so captivating that Radha's anger evaporated just like that. She ran across the hill and took the form of a peahen so that they could dance together.

It is also said that once Krishna and Radha wished to experience love in the form of every species that existed. Krishna started by taking the form of a peacock, and Radha immediately became a peahen. Then he switched to another form of an animal, and she matched him. Again he would switch, and she would follow. Like a whirlwind, they took the form of every species of animal and class of beings in the universe and finally returned to their original forms.

Other stories are also associated with Mayura Kutira. Once, there was a dancing contest judged by Radharani between Krishna and a peacock. Another time, Radha had complained that the forest lacked any beautiful peacocks. Krishna then appeared as a peacock and danced for Radha and her sakhis, her closest companions. Another time, Radha and Krishna had come to the hill together with the other gopis. The peacocks who were there then became ecstatic to see them and started dancing. Clouds gathered in the sky, and a light rain fell.

Radha and Krishna were intoxicated by the beauty surrounding them. They took the form of a peacock and a peahen and danced along with the other peacocks and peahens. The gopis were entranced by the skill of their dancing and began spontaneously singing different kinds of melodies, increasing the enjoyment of Radha and Krishna.

~

A HUNDRED YEARS ago or so, a blind sadhu lived on the hill where the Mayura Kutira was built. He meditated upon this leela of Radha and Krishna from the depths of his heart. He visualized them dancing together as a peacock and a peahen. He could think of nothing else. He longed to be able to see this leela. He performed sadhana with this one wish in his heart.

One day, Radha appeared before him out of compassion.

She told him, "I will reveal to you this leela, but whatever you see you must paint so that others, too, can see this auspicious sight."

The sadhu was eager to do so but worried. "I am blind. How can I see that which I must paint?"

At that time, Barsana Dham was nothing but dense

forest. There was no easy way to obtain a paintbrush or paints.

Radharani assured him that all he had to do was try sincerely. She would take care of the rest. And so it was that by digging in the ground, he collected different minerals that could be transformed into paints. All the other materials also came to him. Even though he could not even see a ray of sunlight, in his mind's eye he saw the full panoramic view of Radha and Krishna dancing as a peahen and a peacock.

Awakening from samadhi, the sadhu faithfully painted that picture, rendering every detail precisely. That painting is present even today on the altar of the temple of Mayura Kutira.

26

The Mock Quarrel of Shiva & Parvati

Once, Shiva and Parvati had a lovers' quarrel. Parvati was upset, and Shiva tried to cheer her up.

Shiva asked, "Devi, why are you upset? Have I done something wrong?"

Parvati sniffed. "My husband, you do not love me anymore."

Shiva harrumphed. "That is not true. Why in the three worlds would you ever think so?"

Parvati replied, "Hmm! These days, you do not bring me the flowers that I love the most."

Shiva smiled. "Oh, so that's what concerns you, is it? My dear, you know that Nandi is not keeping well these days." Nandi was the bull vahana of Shiva. "I have to climb up the hills on his back to fetch those flowers you especially prefer. Trust me, if I make him go with me now, it will not be good for his health."

Parvati conceded that point. "Fine. But you no longer ask me to dance with you."

Shiva's smile turned into a grin. "Devi, you are my wife.

What formality is this that I must invite you. You can dance with me anytime you want."

Parvati's eyes narrowed upon his mouth still curved upwards into that mischievous grin.

"Do not try to fool me. I have noticed that these days you are smiling even when you are meditating. I know you are thinking about someone else and smiling at the thought of her."

Shiva scoffed. "Devi, you are yourself the most accomplished yogini and an enlightened one. You know that meditation arouses inner joy which shows itself on one's face. Why would I not smile during meditation?"

Parvati plowed on. "These days, you leave home early in the morning and return late at night. Where are you off to all day?"

Shiva's eyebrows rose in amusement. It was unlike his wife to nag him. He went along with it, hoping to placate her.

"My dear, you know very well that there are so many people who depend on me. I have to look after them all. You know better than anyone what my responsibilities and burdens are. Come now, tell me what it is that is truly worrying you."

Parvati bit her lip. She was reluctant to confess her true concern. Shiva waited patiently for her to speak. Finally, she gave in and confided in him that which truly plagued her.

"I know what is really going on with you. That Ganga, that beautiful Devi of the most sacred of rivers, sits over your head day and night. That is the real reason you do not love me so much anymore."

Shiva burst out laughing, touched and amused by his wife's jealousy.

"Oh! Ganga! Do not worry about her. She takes up only a small space on my head. How can you compare yourself with her? You are my wife and you and I are halves of the same being."

In that moment, Shiva revealed to Parvati the Ardha-narishvara form, half Shiva and half Parvati. This is yet another story associated with that most sublime and sacred of worship-worthy images and forms, the story with which we started this collection.

Parvati's anger and hurt disappeared at the sight of that special form that was theirs and theirs alone. She leaned into Shiva's embrace, and they relished the marital bliss they shared. Sometimes even the greatest of Devas and Devis argue and quarrel just like mortal couples!

Part Ten

Bhamati

27

Bhamati

I mentioned one day that I would be including the story of Bhamati, the story that follows, in this collection of Hindu Love Stories. My friend was surprised. It did not seem like a love story at all, she said; it did not seem like it would fit.

And yet I can think of no better story with which to end this collection than the story of Bhamati.

This is a story from history, as true and real as history from hundreds of years ago can be. It is a story of Vachaspati Mishra, who became one of the most renowned scholars and acharyas of Advaita Vedanta. In the end, though, his wife's fame eclipsed his own.

When Vachaspati Mishra was a young scholar in the 9th or 10th century living in the area of present-day Mithila, he was committed to becoming a renunciate and taking sannyasa. He wanted to devote his life to writing commentaries on the Brahma Sutras.

His mother, Vatsala, though, was keen to marry him off to a girl from the neighboring village. Vatsala was a single mother who had worked hard to raise him on her own and wanted to ensure he had a secure and comfortable future. She had already broached the subject with the father of the bride.

Vachaspati was completely uninterested. He wrote to the bride's father directly and said that he intended to leave the village and take sannyasa, that he would not make a good householder or husband. A householder should fulfill the responsibilities of family life, and that was not his path.

He wrote, "This is my service to humanity. Those scriptures are dearer to me than my own life. I will not be able to perform the duties of a *grhastha*, a householder. I doubt I would make an adequate husband. There is nothing else in my mind, other than writing the commentaries on the Brahma Sutra. I have even vowed to take sannyasa after I finish writing the commentary."

The bride's father read the letter out loud to his daughter. He decided to not move forward with the engagement. But Bhamati, his daughter, was impressed by Vachaspati's commitment to spirituality and wanted to marry him. She asked her father, to his surprise, to let the wedding proceed.

The bride's father explained this to Vatsala and asked Vachaspati if he would like to meet her.

Vachaspati refused. "She has already chosen me, so I do not have the right to negate her choice."

Vachaspati and Bhamati were married on Guru Purnima, an auspicious day dedicated to honoring and revering one's spiritual preceptor, the guru. As soon as they returned home from the wedding, Vachaspati started writing and forgot all about Bhamati. After all, Guru Purnima was also the most auspicious day on which to start writing his book.

He sat on the verandah and wrote day and night. The months and all passed and changed around him, but he did not even notice. Other than a quick bath, eating a bit of food, and taking a few hours to sleep, he did nothing but read, think, and write.

While Vachaspati Mishra was writing his commentary, Bhamati served him without any expectations. Years passed like this. Sometimes if their paths crossed in the house, he would assume Bhamati was a new maid who worked in the house.

Vachaspati had forgotten that he even had a wife. He did not think to wonder how it was that there were always palm-leaves kept ready at his hand for him to write on, how the lamp was always filled with oil, the cotton wick neatly trimmed, how his clothes were washed and kept fresh for him, how there was a plate of food next to him whenever he felt hungry. He took it all for granted. She even placed flowers at his feet every morning.

One night on a full-moon night like the one on which they had gotten married, after many years had passed, Vachaspati Mishra finally finished writing his book. When he rose to go to bed, his wife picked up the lamp to show him the way. For the first time, Vachaspati saw his wife's hand. He saw her hands, the bangles adorning her wrists, and heard the tinkling of her bracelets.

"Who are you?" he asked. "What are you doing here so late at night?"

"I am Bhamati, your wife. You have been so immersed in writing your book that you have forgotten that you married me many years ago."

Some say seven years had passed; others that twelve years had passed; still others say eighteen years had passed like this. Whatever the true number of years may be, it had definitely been a very long time.

Vachaspati asked, "Then was it you who placed flowers at my feet each morning? And was it you who put the tray before me and was it you who lit the lamp for me every evening? But how is it that I did not ever see your hand?"

Bhamati replied, "If my hand had become visible to you, it would perhaps have disturbed your concentration. It would have meant that my love was lacking. I could keep waiting."

Vachaspati was shocked. How could it be that for so many years she had been looking after his every need, yet he had never even seen her. Not only that, she had deliberately kept her presence as unobtrusive as possible so as not to distract him. Tears rolled down his eyes.

Bhamati told him that she had no complaints. She was proud to be married to someone like him and was blessed to have been able to associate with him in completing that great work which would be of such great service to humanity in times to come.

Memories from the past started flowing into Vachaspati's mind.

"Yes, yes, I remember now. Show me your hands."

She held out her hands to him.

Vachaspati looked at her hands. He said in a voice tinged with regret, "These hands have been placing the lamp by my side and serving me my dinner every day after sunset. I know these hands, though I had not recognized them before. But now it is too late, as I have taken a vow that the day I finish my commentaries I would take sannyasa and leave this village!"

Bhamati nodded serenely. She had already known this would happen.

Vachaspati expressed his gratitude to her in a choked voice.

"You are a rare woman," was all he could manage to say,

that eloquent scholar who had authored such a great commentary on the Brahma Sutra.

Bhamati remained calm. "Do not worry. I will never come in your way."

Vachaspati was overcome. "There could be many commentators like me, but there will only be one of you. Nobody could find a woman of your quality, with such unconditional love, such patience, such purity and magnanimity of heart. I shall name my book 'Bhamati' so that whosoever reads it will remember you and honor you."

He said to her, as a tribute to his great wife's sacrifices: "All I have—my life goal, my karma, my life's work, the very meaning and purpose of my life—I am surrendering it at your feet. Still, I cannot think of anything I can give that will match your love."

He worried about what would happen to her when he was gone.

"How will you look after yourself? What will you do, my Devi, when I am gone?"

He wept for her.

She smiled. "That very force that brought you to me and gave me the opportunity to serve you will watch over me. Your devotion and sincerity towards your spirituality and work will always inspire me. Whatever I was to achieve, I have achieved through these tears of yours. I wish for nothing more. Go without any regret. What more could I have achieved than this, that Vachaspati's eyes are filled with tears for me?"

Vachaspati became a renunciate and left for the Himalayas.

While there have been written many great commentaries on the Brahma Sutra, the Bhamati Tika is considered one of the greatest in all of Advaita Vedanta. Vachaspati

Mishra would go on to found one of the main schools of Advaita Vedanta, which became known as the Bhamati school. Today, more people know the name of Bhamati than know the name of Vachaspati Mishra. That is how he would have wanted it.

He had said to her, "I can do nothing for you but let the world forget me. Let it not forget you."

Afterword

Why is it that the story of Bhamati is one of my favorites? After all, it is bittersweet and it seems, if not unfair, since Bhamati did go into the marriage with eyes wide open, asymmetrical and inequitable. It is impossible to not sympathize with her, this young woman so in love with her elder husband, this bride who puts his dream and ambition not just above her own but in place of her own. If we were to ask that young woman whether she would have preferred to have her husband's company and love throughout their lifetime together or to have a famous and important philosophical text named after her, we can guess that in her heart of hearts she probably would have wished for the former. But she willingly sacrificed that for the sake of her beloved.

That volition, that willingness, that agency is key — without that, it would just be coercion and victimization which must never be glorified or honored.

We have become so conditioned to think of love as being centered on our own gratification and enjoyment that we have come to take it as an entitlement. Life is unbearably boring if we do not always have this addictive high of pleasure and fulfillment. It has become a battleground on which we seek equality and fairness, perfect reciprocity. All this confusion we have about love, this mishmash of sentimentality and neediness, all of this is as delusional as it is to believe in those fairy tales that end in happily-ever-after.

As Hemalekha, she of Tripura Rahasya, would tell us,

'When I think about it, no one seems to possess enough of anything to provide for lasting happiness. That which will one day provide misery, on account of being insufficient to provide happiness any longer, cannot be said to be a source of happiness. The satisfaction from the fulfillment of a desire before another desire takes its place cannot be said to be happiness, since the seeds of future pain are still latent.'

We have come to resent sacrifice nowadays, seeing it as something we are forced to give up, as something that we give away of ourselves, something that takes away from us. Yet in Dharma, sacrifice is that which makes us stronger, that which sustains the entire cycle and circle of life.

Sri Krishna, in the third adhyaya, or chapter, of the Bhagavad Gita discourses at length about the importance of sacrifice:

> ajnaarthaat karmano'nyatra loko'yam
>   karmabandhanah;
> Tadartham karma kaunteya muktasangah
>   samaachara.

> 9. The world is bound by actions other than
>   those performed for the sake of sacrifice;
>   do thou, therefore, O son of Kunti,
>   perform action for that sake (for sacri-
>   fice) alone, free from attachment!

Sahayajnaah prajaah srishtwaa purovaacha
  prajaapatih;
Anena prasavishyadhwam esha vo'stvish-
  takaamadhuk.

10. The Creator, having in the beginning of
  creation created mankind together with
  sacrifice, said: "By this shall ye propa-
  gate; let this be the milch cow of your
  desires (the cow which yields the
  desired objects)".

Devaan bhaavayataanena te devaa
  bhaavayantu vah;
Parasparam bhaavayantah shreyah param
  avaapsyatha.

11. With this do ye nourish the gods, and
  may the gods nourish you; thus nour-
  ishing one another, ye shall attain to the
  highest good.
Ishtaan bhogaan hi vo devaa daasyante
  yajnabhaavitaah;
Tair dattaan apradaayaibhyo yo bhungkte
  stena eva sah.
  ...

Annaad bhavanti bhootaani parjanyaad
  anna sambhavah;
Yajnaad bhavati parjanyo yajnah karma
  samudbhavah.

14. From food come forth beings, and from

rain food is produced; from sacrifice
arises rain, and sacrifice is born of
action.

...

Evam pravartitam chakram naanuvartaya-
    teeha yah;
Aghaayur indriyaaraamo mogham paartha
    sa jeevati.

16. He who does not follow the wheel thus
    set revolving, who is of sinful life,
    rejoicing in the senses, he lives in vain,
    O Arjuna![1]

Without sacrifice, without the making of offerings, the underlying harmony, order, and balance of Rtam is disturbed. Rtam is impossible to define but in essence it is the natural order of the cosmos that regulates and coordinates the working of the various orders and dimensions of existence.

This conception of sacrifice can and should be understood at different levels of meaning. At the literal level, these verses speak to the importance of observing the prescribed rites, such as the performance of Agnihotra, the daily fire sacrifice to be performed by householders. At a more philosophical level, it also speaks to our attitudes to all the actions we take in our life. Each human being is obligated to undertake the pancha-mahayajna, the daily five-fold sacrifice to be offered to the Devas, the rishis, the ancestors, humanity, and all sentient beings. At the highest of levels, we can offer our thought, speech and physical movements as sacrifice also.

Nor is the performance of sacrifice about the abnegation of the self in favor of the other. This kind of thinking reflects a crudeness that has crept into us because we have become conditioned to thinking of love in transactional terms, in the gratification of our desire in exchange for gratifying someone else's. This results in relationships becoming a negotiation, a constantly adversarial interaction resulting in bartering rather than freely sharing. Rather, what Dharma points us to is seeing ourselves a part of the whole and seeking always to optimize the wellbeing of the whole.

There is a practical application to this, a corollary that we can see in the corporate world. Many studies have found that women underperform men when it comes to negotiating for things like promotions or raises in the workplace. A simple change in perspective, though, produces a radical change. When women negotiate for the same kinds of things but now on behalf of their team or their family, their performance matches if not exceeds that of men.

What relevance then do these stories from thousands or hundreds of years ago hold for us today? Is it that we are expected to become like Savitri or Bhamati or Vishnupriya Devi? Is it that we should, like Ruru, give up half of our lifetimes for the sake of our beloved?

No, that would be too simplistic. Rather, it is to understand and appreciate that these ideals exist, that there is another way to conceive of and approach love, one that leads us closer to enlightenment and self-realization, that brings us contentment and gratitude rather than the dizzying peaks and valleys of an emotional rollercoaster that wreaks havoc with our psyche and self-esteem. And to find inspiration and motivation from these legendary and iconic figures without necessarily imitating them.

Perhaps we can be a little bit like Lopamudra and be

frank and open about our desires and longing. Perhaps we can be like Hemachuda and learn to look upon our lovers not just as objects of desire but as partners who can teach us a thing or two. Perhaps like Queen Leela we can learn that we must sometimes go beyond attachment, to understand that there is no fundamental reality to the conceptions of relationship and bondage upon which we build our lives and identity. Perhaps we can use love to make ourselves better and to make each other better, too — perhaps we can rise through love instead of falling into it.

Notes

2. Vishnu & Lakshmi

1. Dimmitt, Cornelia. *Classical Hindu Mythology: A Reader in the Sanskrit Puranas*. United States: Temple University Press, 2012, p. 99.
2. *See* Horace Hayman Wilson, trans., *The Vishnu Purana*, Book I: Chapter IX - Legend of Lakshmi (website), last updated on November 9, 2018, https://www.wisdomlib.org/hinduism/book/vishnu-purana-wilson/d/doc115945.html.

4. Agni & Swaha

1. Brereton, Joel., Jamison, Stephanie. The Rigveda: A Guide. United States: Oxford University Press, 2020, p. 89.

7. Menaka & Vishwamitra

1. Goethe, Johann. *Goethe's Works, vol. 1 (Poems)*. Philadelphia: G. Barrie, 1885. https://oll.libertyfund.org/title/boyesen-goethe-s-works-vol-1-poems.

8. Pururavas & Urvashi

1. Joel Brereton, Stephanie Jamison, *The Rigveda: A Guide* (New York: Oxford University Press, 2020), 1549.
2. Joel Brereton, Stephanie Jamison, *The Rigveda: A Guide* (New York: Oxford University Press, 2020), 1549.
3. Joel Brereton, Stephanie Jamison, *The Rigveda: A Guide* (New York: Oxford University Press, 2020), 1550.
4. Joel Brereton, Stephanie Jamison, *The Rigveda: A Guide* (New York: Oxford University Press, 2020), 1550.

9. Agastya & Lopamudra

1. Joel Brereton, Stephanie Jamison, *The Rigveda: A Guide* (New York: Oxford University Press, 2020), 380.

11. Usha & Aniruddha

1. Swami Tapasyananda, trans., *Srimad Bhagavata: The Holy Book of God* (Chennai, India: Sri Ramakrishna Math, 1980), 3:745.
2. Swami Tapasyananda, trans., *Srimad Bhagavata: The Holy Book of God* (Chennai, India: Sri Ramakrishna Math, 1980), 3:768.

12. Chyavana & Sukanya

1. Kisari Mohan Ganguli, trans., *The Mahabharata of Krishna-Dwaipayana Vyasa, Translated into English Prose from the original Sanskrit Text* (India: Munshiram Manoharlal Publishers Pvt. Ltd., 1993), 3:260.

13. Satyabhama & Krishna

1. Swami Tapasyananda, trans., *Srimad Bhagavata: The Holy Book of God* (Chennai, India: Sri Ramakrishna Math, 1980), 3:680.

14. Hemachuda & Hemalekha

1. "Chapter II," Tripura Rahasya or The Mystery Beyond the Trinity, Sri Ramanasramam, accessed February 5, 2022, https://scriptures.ru/tripura1.htm#CHAPTER%20II.
2. "Chapter IV," Tripura Rahasya or The Mystery Beyond the Trinity, Sri Ramanasramam, accessed February 5, 2022, https://scriptures.ru/tripura1.htm#CHAPTER%20IV.
3. "Chapter X," Tripura Rahasya or The Mystery Beyond the Trinity, Sri Ramanasramam, accessed February 5, 2022, https://scriptures.ru/tripura1.htm#CHAPTER%20X.

15. Chaitanya Mahaprabhu & Vishnupriya Devi

1. "Vishnupriya Devi — Biography", Gaudiya History, ISKCON Desire Tree, accessed February 6, 2022.
2. "Dhameshvar Mahaprabhu's Temple", ISKCON Desire Tree, ISKCON Desire Tree, accessed February 6, 2022, https://iskcondesiretree.com/page/dhameshvar-mahaprabhu-s-temple.

16. Bilvamangala Thakur & Chintamani

1. Mahanidhi Swami, *Gaudiya Vaishnava Biographies and Samadhis in Vrndavana*, 2013, Kindle.

17. Leela & Padma

1. Swami Venkatesananda, *Vasistha's Yoga* (Albany: State University of New York Press, 1993), 58-59.
2. Swami Venkatesananda, *Vasistha's Yoga* (Albany: State University of New York Press, 1993), 60.
3. Swami Venkatesananda, *Vasistha's Yoga* (Albany: State University of New York Press, 1993), 65.
4. Swami Venkatesananda, *Vasistha's Yoga* (Albany: State University of New York Press, 1993), 71.

19. Ruru & Pramadvara

1. Kisari Mohan Ganguli, *The Mahabharata of Krishna-Dwaipayana Vyasa, Translated into English Prose from the Original Sanskrit Text*, India: Munshiram Manoharlal Publishers Pvt. Ltd., 2015, 1:53.

21. The Story of the Crow

1. V.S. Srinivasa Sastri, *Lectures on the Ramayana*, (Madras: Madras Sanskrit Academy, 2006), 23–24, 26.
2. Adapted from: K.M.K. Murthy, "Sarga 38, Sundara Kanda", Valmiki Ramayana, accessed on February 7, 2022, https://www.valmikiramayan.net/utf8/sundara/sarga38/sundara_38_frame.htm.

23. Separation in Union: The Two Bees

1. Translation adapted from "Chapter 46, Delivery of the Message of Krsna to the Gopis," *Krsna, The Supreme Personality of Godhead* (website), His Divine Grace A.C. Bhaktivedanta Swami Prabhupada, accessed February 5, 2022, https://krsnabook.com/ch46.html.

Note

1. Brahma Sutra, 2.1.33.

Afterword

1. Swami Sivananda, trans., *The Bhagavad Gita*, (Tehri-Garhwal, India: Divine Life Trust Society: 2000 (website)), accessed on February 7, 2022, https://www.dlshq.org/download/bhagavad-gita/#_VPID_12.

Bibliography

Ardhanarishvara

Nagar, Shanti Lal, trans. *Siva Mahapurana* (*An Exhaustive Introduction, Sanskrit Text, English Translation with Photographs of Archaeological Evidence*). Delhi: Parimal Publications, 2007.

Tagare, G.V., trans. *The Skanda Purana* (website), last updated on April 16, 2021. https://www.wisdomlib.org/hinduism/book/the-skanda-purana.

Vishnu & Lakshmi

Wilson, Horace Hayman, trans. *The Vishnu Purana*, Book I: Chapter IX - Legend of Lakshmi (website), last updated on November 9, 2018. https://www.wisdomlib.org/hinduism/book/vishnu-purana-wilson/d/doc115945.html.

The Birth of Radha as a Blind Girl

This story is found in folklore and the oral tradition. References can be found in a few different books, including the following: Das, R.K. *Temples of Vrindaban*. India: Sandeep Prakashan, 1990.

Agni & Swaha

Ganguli, Kisari Mohan, trans. *The Mahabharata of Krishna Dwaipayana Vyasa, Translated into English Prose from the Original Sanskrit Text*. India: Munshiram Manoharlal Publishers Pvt. Ltd., 2015.

The Two Wives of Skanda

Ganguli, Kisari Mohan, trans. *The Mahabharata of Krishna Dwaipayana Vyasa, Translated into English Prose from the Original Sanskrit Text*. India: Munshiram Manoharlal Publishers Pvt. Ltd., 2015.

Sivaraman, Akila, trans. *Sri Kandha Puranam (English)*. India: GIRI Trading Agency Private, 2006.

Rukmini & Krishna

Swami Tapasyananda, trans. *Srimad Bhagavata: The Holy Book of God*. (Chennai, India: Sri Ramakrishna Math, 1980).

Menaka & Vishwamitra

Ganguli, Kisari Mohan, trans. *The Mahabharata of Krishna Dwaipayana Vyasa, Translated into English Prose from the*

Original Sanskrit Text. (India: Munshiram Manoharlal Publishers Pvt. Ltd., 2015).

Mani, Vettam. *Puranic Encyclopaedia: A Comprehensive Work with Special Reference to the Epic and Puranic Literature*. (Delhi, India: Motilal Banarsidass Publishers Private Limited, 2015).

Pururavas & Urvashi

Brereton, Joel, Stephanie Jamison. *The Rigveda: A Guide*. (New York: Oxford University Press, 2020).

Ganguli, Kisari Mohan, trans. *The Mahabharata of Krishna Dwaipayana Vyasa, Translated into English Prose from the Original Sanskrit Text*. (India: Munshiram Manoharlal Publishers Pvt. Ltd., 2015).

Mani, Vettam. *Puranic Encyclopaedia: A Comprehensive Work with Special Reference to the Epic and Puranic Literature*. (Delhi, India: Motilal Banarsidass Publishers Private Limited, 2015).

Agastya & Lopamudra

Brereton, Joel, Stephanie Jamison. *The Rigveda: A Guide*. (New York: Oxford University Press, 2020).

Ganguli, Kisari Mohan, trans. *The Mahabharata of Krishna Dwaipayana Vyasa, Translated into English Prose from the Original Sanskrit Text*. (India: Munshiram Manoharlal Publishers Pvt. Ltd., 2015).

Kamadeva & Rati

Swami Tapasyananda, trans. *Srimad Bhagavata: The Holy Book of God.* (Chennai, India: Sri Ramakrishna Math, 1980).

Usha & Aniruddha

Swami Tapasyananda, trans. *Srimad Bhagavata: The Holy Book of God.* (Chennai, India: Sri Ramakrishna Math, 1980).

Chyavana & Sukanya

Ganguli, Kisari Mohan, trans. *The Mahabharata of Krishna Dwaipayana Vyasa, Translated into English Prose from the Original Sanskrit Text.* (India: Munshiram Manoharlal Publishers Pvt. Ltd., 2015).

Mani, Vettam. *Puranic Encyclopaedia: A Comprehensive Work with Special Reference to the Epic and Puranic Literature.* (Delhi, India: Motilal Banarsidass Publishers Private Limited, 2015).

Satyabhama & Krishna

Chaitanya, Satya trans. "Satyabhama-Narakasura Fight in the Harivamsa," HarivaMsha, edited by P.L. Vaidya, Volume II, Appendices, published by BORI, Section 28A (pages 209-212) (website). Last accessed February 7, 2022. http://mahabharata-resources.org/southern/satyabhama-naraka-fight-trans.html.

Swami Tapasyananda, trans. *Srimad Bhagavata: The Holy Book of God.* (Chennai, India: Sri Ramakrishna Math, 1980).

Hemachuda & Hemalekha

Saraswathi, Ramanananda, trans. "Chapter II." *Tripura Rahasya or The Mystery Beyond the Trinity.* Accessed February 5, 2022. https://scriptures.ru/tripura1.htm#CHAPTER%20II.

Sri Chaitanya Mahaprabhu & Vishnupriya Devi

ISKCON Desire Tree. "Dhameshvar Mahaprabhu's Temple,"
ISKCON Desire Tree. Accessed February 6, 2022. https://iskcondesiretree.com/page/dhameshvar-mahaprabhu-s-temple.

"Vishnupriya Devi — Biography", Gaudiya History, ISKCON Desire Tree, accessed February 6, 2022, https://gaudiyahistory.iskcondesiretree.com/tag/vishnupriya-devi/.

Bilvamangala Thakur & Chintamani

Mahanidhi Swami. *Gaudiya Vaishnava Biographies and Samadhis in Vrndavana.* 2013. Kindle.

A.C. Bhaktivedanta Swami Prabhupada. "Srimad-Bhagavatam 3.25.32", Srimad-Bhagavatam Lectures. Accessed February 6, 2022. https://prabhupadabooks.com/classes/sb/3/25/32/bombay/december/02/1974.

Leela & Padma

Swami Venkatesananda. *Vasistha's Yoga*. Albany: State University of New York Press, 1993.

Savitri

Ganguli, Kisari Mohan, trans. *The Mahabharata of Krishna Dwaipayana Vyasa, Translated into English Prose from the Original Sanskrit Text*. (India: Munshiram Manoharlal Publishers Pvt. Ltd., 2015).

Ruru & Pramadvara

Ganguli, Kisari Mohan, trans. *The Mahabharata of Krishna Dwaipayana Vyasa, Translated into English Prose from the Original Sanskrit Text*. (India: Munshiram Manoharlal Publishers Pvt. Ltd., 2015).

The Dust of the Gopis' Feet

A.C. Bhaktivedanta Swami Prabhupada. "Lecture on SB 1.8.48", Srimad-Bhagavatam Lectures (website). Last accessed February 7, 2022. https://vaniquotes.org/wiki/The_gopis_gave_the_dust_of_their_feet_for_curing_Krsna%27s_headache

The Story of the Crow

V.S. Srinivasa Sastri, *Lectures on the Ramayana*, (Madras: Madras Sanskrit Academy, 2006), 23–24, 26.

Gita Press. *Srimad Valmiki Ramayana With Sanskrit Text and English Translation.* Gorakhpur, India: Gita Press, 2006.

The Grief of Shiva

Vettam Mani. *Puranic Encyclopaedia: A Comprehensive Work with Special Reference to the Epic and Puranic Literature.* (Delhi, India: Motilal Banarsidass Publishers Private Limited, 2015).

Separation in Union: The Two Bees

Gosvāmī, Śrīla Rūpa., Ṭhākura, Śrīla Viśvanātha Cakrava., Swami, HH Bhanu. Vidagdha Mādhava. N.p.: Amazon Digital Services LLC - KDP Print US, 2018.

Swami Tapasyananda, trans. *Srimad Bhagavata: The Holy Book of God.* (Chennai, India: Sri Ramakrishna Math, 1980).

Union in Separation: A Story of Rukmini, Radha & Krishna

Gargacharya. *Garga Saṁhita.* India: Rasbihari Lal & Sons, 2006.

Peacock Leela

"Barsana-Mayura kutir / Mor kuti." Last accessed February 7, 2022. https://brajdhamooo.wordpress.com/barsana-mayura-kutir-mor-kuti/.

"Morkuti Pastimes." Last accessed February 7, 2022. https://brajrasik.org/articles/ 585f1ed2283dcc7a480eeb92/mor-kuti-braj-divine-pastimes.

The Mock Quarrel of Shiva and Parvati

Jaishree, Manish. "Shiva as Ardhanarishvara". Last accessed February 7, 2022. https://manishjaishree.com/shiva-as-ardhanarishvara/#Ardhanarishvara_form_of_Shiva_8211_r esult_of_spousal_jealousy.

Bhamati

Pai, Udaylal. "Bhamati — True Story of an Ideal Beloved Wife." Last accessed February 7, 2022. https://udaypai.in/ bhamati-true-story-of-an-ideal-beloved-wife/.

"The Bhamati and Vivarana Schools." Last accessed February 7, 2022. https://www.advaita-vedanta.org/ avhp/bhavir.html.

Acknowledgments

In my puja room in a place of the highest honor there is a pair of Padukas (wooden clogs). They belonged once to Sri Abhinava Vidyateertha Mahaswami (1917-1989), Jyeshta Mahasannidhanam and 35th Shankaracharya of Sringeri. Sringeri is one of the four apex Hindu Mathas established by Sri Adi Shankaracharya Bhagavatpada. He was one of the 6 or 8 greatest philosophers the world has ever known. In the Indic Vedic Hindu and associated religious traditions such as Buddhism, Jainism et.al., such padukas are considered objects of immense spiritual energy if you are so karmically fortunate to have them come your way. Every morning, when I sit for sadhana, I feel the flow of blessings to me from those Padukas. Without His Holiness's grace, this little inspirational publication would not have been written.

My book would not have been possible without the blessings and guidance of my diksha guru, Bhagavat Bhaskara Pandit Krishna Chandra Sastri-ji, popularly known as Thakurji, and my siksha guru over the decades, Sri Nagendra S. Rao. Thakurji is one of India's most renowned Bhagavat Saptah exponents, Sanskrit scholar, classical musician and a Ramanuja (Visisht Advaita) Sampradaya authority. Sri Nagendra is of the Shankaracharya (Advaita) Sampradaya and free-standing personal sishya of Jyestha Mahasannidhanam. Any knowledge that I have comes through their grace. Anything I have slightly understood about Dharma, sadhana, and the world-view and ethos of the Itihaasas and Puranas, the source texts for the lore contained in this book, come from them and through the anugraha of Bhagavan Sri Krishna - Srila Radharani, my ishta devatas.

Last but not least, there is a great Vedantin, polymath scholar, yoga siddha, and bhakta who resides silent and unknown, mostly in samadhi, in Chennai. He prefers it that way! He too is a personal sishya of Jyestha Mahasannid-hanam of Sringeri. He gave me three instructions over my life to date over some 20 years. His darshana once for a few precious minutes has been one of the greatest blessings of my life. That little bit of instruction has been enough to transform my life; I hope only to one day be worthy of what I have received from that great soul. Just thinking of him is enough to make my heart tranquil and bring tears to my eyes. Just knowing that one such as him exists provides immense succor to the spirit.

My namaskarams and prostrations to each of them, again and again. May this book be but a small offering of gratitude for all that they have bestowed upon me.

Any merits to be found in this book are due to their teachings and blessings; the errors are mine and mine alone.

This book does not belong to me alone. It is also the creation of my husband and partner, Biswajit Malakar. Not only did he design the book cover, but he was also my first reader. He encouraged and supported me as I toiled through nights and weekends to get this completed in a timely fashion while juggling my career. Biswajit did not begrudge me the constant interruptions to our vacation time so that I could finish my research and drafting. The love and care he provides me are as much of an inspiration to me as any of the stories in this book. I am grateful to Iswara in the form of the eternal duo Srila Radharani-Sri Krishna for bringing us together.

The pandemic of the past two years has made me miss my family more than I could imagine. My mother, Shubhra Banerjee, brother and sister-in-law, Amit Banerjee and Shilpa Banerjee, and little beloved nephews, Aneesh and Avi Banerjee, have been unstintingly supportive of my pursuit of writing and delving into Hinduism. It would not have been possible to write this book without the encouragement, love, and support of them all in making my dreams come true.

My father, my Baba, Bhaskar Nath Banerjee, was and will always be my most kindred spirit. All that I have learned of goodness, of what it means to care for and love another person, all of that comes from him.

I am deeply grateful to Aaron Burkholder for his services in editing and proofreading this book. He brought forth order from chaos and made the manuscript immensely more readable and clear, ensuring consistency of style and convention across the different stories.

About the Author

Aditi Banerjee's first novel, *The Curse of Gandhari*, a successful bestseller, was published by Bloomsbury India in September 2019. Her second novel on Shiva and Sati has been slated for publication in 2022 also by Bloomsbury India.

She is a practicing attorney at a Fortune 500 financial services company in the US and has also completed an Executive MBA at Columbia University. She earned a Juris Doctor from Yale Law School and received a B.A. in International Relations, magna cum laude, from Tufts University.

She is a prolific writer and speaker about Hinduism and the Hindu-American experience. She is a member of the Indic Academy and Indic Book Club, which sponsored a successful six-city book launch tour for *The Curse of Gandhari* in September 2019 across India.

She co-edited the book, *Invading the Sacred: An Analysis of Hinduism Studies in America* in collaboration with Rajiv Malhotra, and has authored several essays in publications such as The Columbia Documentary History of Religion in America since 1945 and Buddhists, Hindus, and Sikhs in

America: A Short History (Religion in American Life) (Oxford University Press). Her articles have also been published in *Outlook India* and many other publications.

In her free time, she enjoys wandering the Himalayas, cooking with the latest kitchen gadgets, hunting for that perfect cup of coffee, and reading about history and world literature.

- facebook.com/aditi.banerjee.3576
- twitter.com/Abanero1
- instagram.com/abanero1
- amazon.com/Aditi-Banerjee/e/B07V2ZTBD1?ref=sr_nt-t_srch_lnk_1&qid=1643426967&sr=8-1

Also by Aditi Banerjee

The Curse of Gandhari

Gandhari, the blindfolded queen-mother of the Kauravas, sees through it all...

Gandhari has one day left to live. As she stares death in the face, her memories travel back to the beginning of her story, to life's unfairness at every point: A fiercely intelligent princess who willfully blindfolded herself for the sake of her peevish, visually-impaired husband; who underwent a horrible pregnancy to mother one hundred sons, each as unworthy as the other; whose stern *tapasya* never earned her a place in people's hearts, nor commanded the respect that Draupadi and Kunti attained; who even today is perceived either as an ingratiatingly self-sacrificing wife or a bad mother who was unable to control her sons and was, therefore, partly responsible for the great war of the Mahabharata...

In this insightful and sensitive portrayal, Aditi Banerjee rescues Gandhari from being reduced to a mere symbol of her blindfold. She builds her up, as Veda Vyasa did, as an unconventional heroine of great strength and iron will – who, when crossed, embarked upon a complex relationship with Lord Krishna, and became the queen who cursed a God...

Printed in Great Britain
by Amazon

82397282R00154